DON'T YOU FORGET ABOUT ME

LOVE ON THE RADIO
BOOK 2

NAIMA SIMONE

PROLOGUE

From: Lennon Ward <lennonforever1@gmail.com>
Sent: May 08, 2012 8:49 PM
To: King Sullivan <kingdontgaf@yahoo.com>
Subject: Missed You

Heyyyy,

Well, I did it. I'm officially a high school graduate. And thank God! There were really some days there that I didn't think I'd make it. And if it wasn't for you, King, I might not have. In a way, this night, this degree is as much yours as it is mine. Which, hello? Where were you? I missed you tonight! I know we agreed that Dad couldn't see you or he would lose his mind, but still... I thought I'd see you there as I crossed the stage. I wanted to see you.

You and Mom.

God, I sound like a spoiled brat, don't I? Instead of being thankful for the parent and friends I had there, all I'm focusing on are the ones who were missing. But Mom, she should've been here with us, with me. She's been gone four years, and some days I feel every one of those years. And other days, like today, it seems like four hours. I asked Dad to leave an empty seat for her next to him. He had the extra ticket. He could've done it for me. I mean, it was my day. But he didn't. Because he's...fucking him. And yes, I cursed. But this called for it. One thing. I just asked this one thing from him on my graduation day, and he couldn't do it. No, *wouldn't* do it. I'm so ready to leave Pike's End. Ready to leave with you and begin the life we were meant to have together.

Because I'm so tired, King.

Tired of having to grieve how my dad grieves. Which is not at all.

Tired of having to hide who I am. Tired of having to hide you.

Look at us. Eighteen and twenty year olds in 2012 *emailing* for godsakes. I can't wait until I can text and call you freely without fear of my father tracking the phone bill just to see who I talk to and losing his shit. Again, curse called for.

Anyway, I can talk to you all about this when I see you in a few minutes. I can't wait to see you. I love you so much. And I can't wait to show you just how much.

God. My dirty talk game is so awkward and weird.

Yours forever,

Lennon

From: Lennon Ward <lennonforever1@gmail.com>
Sent: May 09, 2012 12:49 PM
To: King Sullivan <kingdontgaf@yahoo.com>
Subject: Checking on you

HEY, KING,

Just checking in on you. I overheard Dad in his office this morning. Okay, yes, I was eavesdropping. Your brother was arrested last night? I'm so sorry. Now I understand why you didn't meet me last night. Have you talked to Leif yet? Is he okay? I wish I could talk to you, be with you. You must be so scared for Leif right now. Call me when you can, okay? I don't care about my dad finding out. I'm worried about you.

Listen, I know you always turn me down when it comes to money but I have savings. And I planned on bringing it with me when we left for L.A. anyway. So what if we use it a little early to bail Leif out? What's mine is yours because we love each other. Please let me be there for you. Leif means everything to you so he means the same to me.

Okay, I'll wait to hear from you.

Yours forever,

Lennon

From: Lennon Ward <lennonforever1@gmail.com>
Sent: May 12, 2012 4:08 AM
To: King Sullivan <kingdontgaf@yahoo.com>
Subject: Worried

HEY, KING,

Okay, I'm trying not to worry. No, that's a lie. I'm past worried. Now, I'm just trying not to freak out. It's been three days. Leif is out of jail, and I still haven't heard from you or seen you. I drove by your house last night and almost stopped and went in. Just to see... Just to find out... But in the end I kept going. I didn't want to get either one of us in trouble or risk anyone finding out our plans and trying to stop us from leaving. And King, I believe in you. I believe in *us*.

But I can't lie.

It's hard when I haven't heard one word from you in four days. Haven't seen you in five. And yes, I'm counting them. Because, if I don't, I feel like I start to lose myself and it seems longer. God, I miss you. I know it's just been a day, and I cringe even writing this, sounding so needy. Still, I'm missing everything about you. Your body on me. Covering me. Taking me. I'm aching for you, your arms, your touch. It's a physical ache.

Please, King.

Write me. Call me. Text me. Hell, send me a message by pigeon.

I just want to know that you're all right. That we're all right.

And God. Ignore that last part. I sound so pathetic. I know we're fine.

Just call, okay?

Yours forever,

Lennon

From: Lennon Ward <lennonforever1@gmail.com>
Sent: May 18, 2012 11:24 PM
To: King Sullivan <kingdontgaf@yahoo.com>
Subject: Where are you?

KING,

It's been eight days. Eight. Days. I'm past worried and have gone on to fucking afraid.

Where are you?

Leif has been out of jail for nearly a week now and I've seen him downtown and outside of Hunt Auto. And still nothing of you. Nothing *from* you. I'm still trying to hold onto the hope that we're leaving together, that you haven't left me. But, King, I can't lie. Each day that passes, it's getting harder and harder to believe that we'll be together. That you're going to keep your promise to me. That you won't leave me.

But the thought that every time you held me, kissed me, made love to me was a lie makes me sick. I refuse to believe that. You love me just as much as I love you and we swore we'd never abandon each other. No matter what anyone says, I know you'd never do that to me.

So I'll wait for you.

I'll trust you.

Please, please don't break my heart, King.

Yours forever,

Lennon

From: Lennon Ward <lennonforever1@gmail.com>
Sent: June 1, 2012 12:24 AM
To: King Sullivan <kingdontgaf@yahoo.com>
Subject: Gone

YOU'RE GONE. I'VE BEEN IN DENIAL ABOUT IT, BUT I can't any longer. I tried. Even though the proof stared me in the face that you were no longer in Pike's End, I still denied it. But I did something we promised each other that we wouldn't do. I went to your house last night. Yes, I broke a promise, but to be fair, you broke yours to me first.

Desperation, worry, anger, fear.

All of them drove me to your house, screw the consequences. Your father answered the door, and he told me what a part of me knew all along but was too scared to admit to myself—you left. You left *me*.

I couldn't even ask him how long, because in the end, it doesn't matter, does it? It could be the night of my graduation, two days later or yesterday. The result is the same. You're gone and I'm here. Alone. Without you. Something you vowed I'd never be.

Am I pathetic for hoping you'll come back for me?

I feel pathetic. I feel sad and like an ass but I'm still fucking hopeful. Even though my every fear has come to life, I still can't claw out the hope that refuses to leave my heart.

Because I know you love me. No matter what the circumstances look like right now, I know *we* can't be a lie. Every moment, every second just can't be.

But I'm so damn terrified it is.

If you ever cared about me... If I ever mattered to you, King, please... Please, call me. Email me.

Do...something.

Yours,

Lennon

From: Lennon Ward <lennonforever1@gmail.com>
Sent: July 6, 2012 9:11 PM
To: King Sullivan <kingdontgaf@yahoo.com>
Subject: Fuck you

FUCK. YOU, KING SULLIVAN.

I got your note from Leif.

And you're a liar. A liar and a coward.

God, how did I ever believe a word you said to me?

Now, in hindsight, I'm kind of thankful we didn't tell anyone about us. The only thing that would've made this worse is if everyone knew how you played me. Or maybe that's what you planned all along. To use me in your fucked up game to pay back everyone in this town for imagined slights against you. Was that all I was to you? One last, giant fuck you before leaving for good?

Well, fuck you right back.

Fuck you for making me believe in you.

Fuck you for making me love you.

You probably won't read this either. Or if you do, you won't have the balls to respond to it. And that's fine. This is more for me anyway because you had your say in that letter.

I don't need you, King. I don't want you. And I don't love you, just as you never loved me. Because if you did, you couldn't hurt me like this. You couldn't just walk away without a backward glance, without one word.

Congratulations, King. You won. You wanted to get rid of me, mission accomplished. I won't email, call or text you again. I'm done making a fool of myself over you.

I'm just done.

Never yours,

Lennon

1

TEN YEARS LATER

Lennon

"King Sullivan is back."

I freeze, my hand clutching my forkful of homemade macaroni 'n' cheese like it's a steadily unraveling rope dangling over a sheer cliff.

And no, I'm not being dramatic.

My grip is that desperate. That frantically hopeful.

Because with those four casually tossed words from my father, I've gone from standing on steady, firm ground to hanging on for dear life with nothing but pebbles and sky beneath my bicycling feet.

So no. When your father mentions the return of the man who broke your heart into so many pieces the fine grains could fill an hourglass, it's entirely fair to be a little...emotional.

"Lennon?"

I deliberately loosen my death hold from around the fork and lower it to my plate. Reaching for the glass of Cabernet Sauvignon, I pick it up and deliberately take a long sip. Only then, do I meet Dad's steady, dark brown gaze.

"Yes?" Damn. Is that my voice? Scratchy, a little tremulous?

No. *No.*

It's been ten long years. King Sullivan should not —will not—elicit this reaction from me. He's taken more than enough from me. I won't allow him to have my composure, my peace, my calm. He will not have it.

"Did you hear what I said?"

"I did," I say, taking another sip of the wine. And refuse to consider that it might be liquid courage. "You said King Sullivan" the name is bitter and grimy on my tongue like cigarette ash, "is back in town."

Forcing myself to adopt a nonchalance that is a figment of my imagination, I grasp my fork again and lift the abandoned macaroni 'n' cheese to my mouth. Though it's my mother's recipe and my favorite thing in the world to eat, it now sits like a lump of coal on my tongue. Still, I force myself to chew and swallow, because Dad's gaze hasn't wavered. Like he's searching my face for a hidden truth as if I'm a defendant in his courtroom.

"That's right. Just drove right through downtown as bold as a peacock. He and his entourage. As if no one here owns a television or has the internet." He snorts, cutting into his roast with a shake of his head. The corner of his mouth curls, and not even pushing food between his lips and chewing can dislodge the distaste and disapproval marring his expression. "Drugs. Alcohol. So-called rehab can't fix what's in his blood, his genes. Forget the apple not falling far from the tree. That one hasn't even dropped from the branch. Like father, like son. And no amount of money or fame is going to make me or a lot of other people in this town forget exactly who he is."

My stomach folds in on itself, twisting in pain—in protest. Yes, King took advantage of naïve eighteen-year-old me. Hurt me in ways that I claim I'm fully over and healed from. Yet, with just his song on the radio or a flash of his image on the television or computer, and that healing felt more like a practical joke.

A joke that's on me.

It's not fair that a man with a heart not even the sturdiest ice pick could chip away... A man who has indulged in every sin, corruption and overindulgence... A man who seems to have his autopilot set on self-destruction...doesn't show that wear and tear on his fallen angel face, his artist's masterpiece body, that wondrously, tragic and haunting voice. No, in ten years of hard living and harder partying, that beautiful half-boy, half-man grew into a stunning, physically unflawed man.

Seeing an image of him is like self-flagellation to my soul.

Safe to say I hate King Sullivan.

Yet, hearing Dad trash him like King and his father, John, are pieces of shit that should be tossed in a manure pile, causes a different kind of fire to flare in my belly.

Anger.

But not at King.

At Dad. The urge to snap, *You don't know what you're talking about*, rises within me so swift and hard I almost sway beneath its power. To snarl, *What was that about casting the first stones? Because we all have vices, don't we, Dad?*

Vices and skeletons. But Terrance Ward tended to conveniently forget that when he had a boulder to throw at someone else's glass house.

But I swallow the vitriolic words that would

damage the relationship we've built stone by stone, brick by brick over the last decade. The fact is, I lost Mom to death. King abandoned me. Dad has been the only person who has stuck; he never left me, either involuntarily or voluntarily. Sometimes he can absolutely frustrate me with his overprotectiveness and elitist attitude when it comes to certain people, but I love him. He's all I have left.

Still...

I say, "As far as I know, John Sullivan was sober for the better part of seven years before he passed." Not long after King left. "And Leif has stayed out of trouble as well. He's been a long time employee of Hunt Auto for a decade, too."

"Hmph." Dad grunts, forking more pot roast into his mouth. That sour expression doesn't ease. "John was an alcoholic for the better part of twenty years. A few years on the wagon didn't negate his past. All it would've taken was one drink for him to be right back in the muck where he started. And his sons are right behind him."

"From what I understand, his drinking didn't start until after his wife died," I murmur. "I think if anyone would understand that kind of pain and the need to hide from it, you would."

Because I do. There'd been a period of months after Mom's death when Dad had crawled into a bottle of Scotch after dinner and only dragged himself out in time to head into the office the next morning. He'd been a functioning drunk, but a drunk just the same. The only difference between him and John Sullivan was that my father had people who'd closed ranks around him, hiding his behavior. And that he'd eventually recovered. John just...hadn't. He'd sunk deeper and deeper into his disease.

Yet, that hadn't been the worst thing Dad had done.

And he'd committed his act before Mom had even taken her last, rattling, pain-soaked breath.

"I have nothing in common with that man," Dad snaps, offense heavy in his forbidding tone as his fork clatters to his plate. "And I'm insulted that you would dare to suggest that I do."

Before I can explain that all I *suggested* was he have empathy or compassion, he bulldozes on. As he always does when he doesn't want to discuss a subject any further. I smother a sigh and pick up the bottle of Cabernet Sauvignon and pour wine into my glass. When his eyes narrow on me, I arch an eyebrow. If he expects me to get through this discussion without more alcohol, he's sorely overestimated my patience.

And I teach third graders.

"Besides," my father continues, "in spite of John's questionable parenting, he can't be blamed for King's latest antics. Overdosing and nearly dying in a hotel room. A stint in rehab. Illegitimate children. I'll admit, initially it seemed like he had a promising career going for him. But blood will tell. And he's sabotaged that career in every clichéd way he could." Dad shakes his head, and his chuckle is ugly and abhorrent because it's at the expense of someone else's misery. "I told everyone he wouldn't amount to anything. And look," he waves a hand as if King's faults were splayed out before him in all their jarring, HD glory, "I was right."

"I wonder what Pastor Roy would have to say about your glee at someone else's pain and misfortune." The slick observation slips out before I can contain it.

And shit. Maybe I *do* need to cut back on the wine.

Too late to walk it back now, though.

"Are you sermonizing to me, Lennon?" Dad asks, voice silky smooth. "Because if you are, I would have to wonder why you're defending King."

And this, right here, is what made him such an excellent attorney. His ability to twist a person's words and trip them up, placing them on the defensive. As a judge, he was supposed to be more impartial, but he still had never lost his edge. A part of me believes he never will because he enjoys it too much.

But I'm not in his courtroom, and I'm not one of his witnesses to cross examine. But I'm also not a fool. To "defend" King, as he put it, would betray a past I've managed to conceal from him for over ten years.

Although, staring into his piercing, dark brown gaze, an ominous tingle trips down my spine. Like a warning to tread carefully because I'm playing a cat and mouse game I had no idea I'd been engaged in. And only Dad knows the rules.

Mentally, I shake off that uneasy feeling. This is my father. He can be intense, a little intimidating and stern, but he wouldn't toy with me. Wouldn't lie to me. Not after last time.

"Was I defending him?" I casually toss back at him, swirling my wine. "I believed I was just commenting on your obvious delight in how far he's fallen. I wasn't even aware you knew King well enough to be concerned about the state of his life or the how's and why's regarding his return home."

Poking the bear. Yes, that's what I was doing. But I'd effectively passed the ball back into his court. And he'd either have to admit to the reason behind his antipathy toward King—whether it had anything to do with me—or he'd drop the subject.

Please, God, let it be the latter.

His gaze burns into mine, and it requires every bit of the resolve earned in the fires of teaching precocious and often brutally honest eight-and-nine-year-olds to unflinchingly meet it. Besides, Dad scents weakness a mile away. He'll be all over mine like a junkyard dog on fresh meat, regardless of the fact that I'm his daughter. It's in his nature.

"I'm a judge in this county. It's my business to know everything that happens here. Especially when it's in the best interest of this town." His shoulders don't lose their rigidity, but he returns to his dinner. And so do I, even though my appetite ran screaming out the door twenty minutes ago, and I sincerely doubt it's coming back.

My father picks up his own glass and takes a sip, studying me over the rim. "Speaking of best interest... I saw Justin at the courthouse this morning."

Oh for fuck's sake.

I pinch the bridge of my nose, barely swallowing the groan rolling around in my chest.

"Lennon..."

"Dad." I hold up my hand, palm out, and shake my head for added emphasis. "I don't want to argue about Justin."

"I don't want to argue with you either." Still holding his glass, he leans back in his chair. "But as your father, I have the right to inquire about your life and to offer my guidance if it's warranted."

"Well, it's not warranted. If you spoke with Justin about us breaking up—which, I'm assuming you did —then he should've informed you that it was amicable and we parted as friends. So unless your guidance concerns whether or not proper etiquette demands I purchase a post-breakup gift, then we really don't have anything to talk about."

"Sarcasm is beneath you in this situation," he states, the flint in his voice reflected in his gaze.

And from one second to the next, I revert from a full grown twenty-eight-year-old to the little girl chastised for her "defiance" and "lip." Only recently had remnants of that little girl started emerging again. And I started realizing that "lip" didn't equal "voice." And defiance was just another label for "power." And yet... Even now, years of conditioning that came from seeking my father's approval tug at me, cracking open a door for guilt and embarrassment to creep in. Sometimes all it takes is one criticism from that judge-on-high voice or a single *I raised you better than that* look from his dark eyes, and I fall back in line.

Because somewhere along the line, Dad had figured out one of my greatest fears is losing him. And maybe it's juvenile as hell, but there's a tiny part of me that's certain one disappointment too many will do just that. Drive him away.

And my father isn't above using that fear to his advantage if it pushes his agenda.

Hey, I never said our relationship didn't have its dysfunctions.

"Also if your defensiveness is anything to go by, then you suspect Justin confided in me regarding the end of your relationship. Which isn't this yarn about this break up being mutual or amicable. You can tell that to me or anyone who listens to ease your conscience, but we both know it's not the truth."

I briefly close my eyes. And convince myself that the tightening in my chest isn't hurt or resentment.

Or the need to hunt down my recent ex and

whisper "Snitches get stitches" in his ear while holding the business end of a protractor to his balls.

"I'm not sure what Justin said to you, but while, yes, I initiated the talk between us that was *long* past due, he agreed that our time together as a couple had come to an end. Four years and we weren't progressing forward. We"

"And whose fault was that?" he snaps.

"Ours since it requires two people to be in a relationship," I reply through clenched teeth. Then, I pause. Count to fifteen and add another five just to be on the safe side. "I understand Justin is your friend, but I can't force feelings I don't have or waste more years in a dead-end relationship just because he's your friend."

Dad's chin snaps back toward his neck. "Oh so now it's my fault that you couldn't make it work?"

Lord, give me strength. And if there's any way you could turn wine into whiskey...? I mean, you turned water into wine. It's the next obvious step...

Jesus is obviously too busy elsewhere because my Cabernet Sauvignon isn't pulling a transfiguration act. Got it. I'm on my own.

Figures. I'm used to my prayers going unanswered.

Please, let my mother live.

Please, bring King back to me.

Please, let me never see King again.

At this point, prayers are just based on habit not faith.

Sighing, I pick up my non-whiskey and sip from it. A *long* sip.

"No, Dad, that's not what I'm saying." I hold onto the glass instead of putting it back down on the table. Who am I kidding. I'm going to need it again shortly.

"But Justin and I probably stayed together longer than we should've because he's your friend and respects you. And he's one of the very few men I've dated that you've actually approved of. Neither one of us wanted to disappoint you. But I can't allow that to dictate my decisions any longer."

"That's ridiculous." He waves his fork before jabbing it in my direction. "Of course you can." I suck in a shocking breath of air that slicks ice over my lungs. My spine goes ramrod straight, and I blink. Then blink again. Before I can squeeze a word past my constricted throat, he continues. "Where do children get the idea that they shouldn't consider other people, especially their parents and loved ones, in their decisions, their actions. After all, you aren't the only ones who will be directly affected by them. We will, too. To not consider others is just selfish and immature."

"Dad," I murmur.

"No, don't 'Dad' me." He shoves a scoop of macaroni 'n' cheese in his mouth, chews, then rolls on with his lecture. "I'm older, have seen more than you and am wiser just from experience alone. I can see around corners you can't. You're twenty-eight, Lennon. And while teaching is a noble job, you need to have a husband and a family. Justin, with a steady career with the potential for political appointments, is the perfect man. He's stable, wealthy in his own right, comes from a great, respected family, and will be able to provide for you and your children. Who else is better than him in Pike's End? You're being very short-sighted and impulsive in this decision."

He states this as if his pronouncement should be accompanied by two stone tablets and a non-bushburning fire. But that's the problem. In this town,

Judge Terrance Ward's word is law. And he believes he's some kind of deity to me.

And I've let him nurture that belief. For far too long. It was easier than fighting.

Not tonight, though. If I exhibit even the slightest sign of weakness, I'll be wedded, bedded and scheduling Mommy and Me days at the community center, my employment at Pike's End Elementary School nothing but a hazy, bittersweet dream.

No. I love my father. But I won't enter into a loveless marriage where Justin and I will not only make each other miserable, but also any children we have. I won't do it.

"Dad," I say, meeting his gaze and pouring a firmness into my voice that, honestly, is more smoke and mirrors than truth. "I love you. And we're going to table this conversation, agree to disagree and leave it at that. I want to finish our dinner and end this evening on a good note, not a negative one. Now," I set my glass down and picked up my fork, intent on making it through this meal with no more shade, arguments or unsolicited advice. "What were you saying about your day?"

He stares at me through narrowed eyes, and his lips fold in on themselves before he resumes eating.

"It was pretty light. Which is surprising considering the closer we get to the holidays, the more people seem to lose their minds. They're probably just winding up..."

He goes on, and I quietly loose a sigh of relief.

Thankful he let it go.

Thankful he hadn't gone back to the subject of King Sullivan.

Because the only subject I want to avoid more than Justin is my former, secret boyfriend. The boyfriend who'd shattered my heart, stolen my trust in people and destroyed the fragments of my faith.

Yes, I'm very thankful. Now if I can only dodge the man himself as skillfully as I did this conversation.

One can pray.

Or not.

2

King

"Explain to me again how we let you convince us to move to Bumfuck, Washington? Because I must've been drunk as a muthafucka when I agreed to this. Either that or high off good pussy."

I glance over at Kade Gibson, Bloody Sunday's drummer, and kick at the edge of the table his long legs and bare feet are propped up on. Damn. I just moved into this house. Like, today. It still has brand new house smell on it and he's treating it like his flop house. Case in point... I aim a pointed look at the blunt he just plucked from his shirt pocket.

Wincing, he slips it back in his pocket.

"Sorry, bruh." He grunts, dropping his feet to the floor and picking up his tumbler of whiskey. "My bad. I wasn't even thinking." He holds his glass up and light from the suspension lamps hanging from the beamed ceiling reflects off the amber liquid. "This okay?"

"Don't be an ass. Just because I have a problem with it doesn't mean all of you need to stop drinking or smoking, for that matter. Last time I checked, weed was legal in Washington." I snort, waving him off.

But I can't brush off the guilt so easily. It crouches within my chest like a venomous snake, coiled and ready to strike. Ready to sink its fangs deep into muscle, tendon and even bone, spreading shame and humiliation until I'm riddled with it. Breathe it.

My addictions, my demons, my fucking weakness damn near destroyed us all. Nearly devastated the career we'd spent eight years creating, growing. Nearly rendered all of our astronomical success to shit on the soles of my feet. *My feet.* Because it'd been all me.

Trashing hotel rooms. Getting thrown out of clubs for being a high and drunken mess. Images of me, half-naked, with women sprawled over me, damn near out of my mind on drugs, splashed across the blogs and tabloid websites. Showing up late or sleeping through drops and press junkets. Performing high.

I'd become the rock star cliché and was too fucked up to give a damn about the music, my career, my band...my life. The label had put up with my shit until that night.

Until the night I overdosed in the bedroom of that hotel penthouse, people I didn't know and who didn't give a fuck about me outside of what I could provide them—money, second-hand fame, drugs, my dick— partying on while I died.

I scrub a hand down my face, my beard abrading my palm. Yeah, I don't kid myself. Bad press more than true concern had my label slapping down an ultimatum on me while I lay in that hospital bed. Rehab or I was done. And not just me. But Kade, Mac and Gideon.

It'd been a surprisingly easy decision.

Now, six months sober, I have even more reasons to be thankful for my decision. More reasons to protect my sobriety like a dragon guarding its treasure.

Gunner.

"Do what you want. Just no smoking in the house. Gunner..." I add as way of explanation.

And it's enough. I don't need to say anything else.

Kade immediately nods. He, like Mac and Gideon, loves my son nearly as much as I do.

Which is funny as hell when I think about it. None of us ever pictured ourselves as fathers any time soon especially me. Very recent ex-addict front men of rock bands teetering on the edge of burn-out just don't make for good daddy material on paper.

Yet, here we are.

"And you were stone cold sober when I told the three of you I was moving here—from alcohol and pussy. Also, as I recall, I didn't convince you of shit. You damn near insisted on coming with me."

Kade squints, wagging the thick tumbler back and forth at me. "Nah. If I didn't see you living like Jesus with my own two eyes, I'd check your pupils right now. Because that's straight bullshit." The smirk riding the corner of his mouth as he tips the whiskey to his mouth contradicts his irritated grunt.

I duck my head, reaching for my bottle of apple juice, my new favorite drink since getting out of rehab. But Kade has been my friend for too long—almost from the moment me and my piece of shit Mustang rode into L.A.—to not see the gesture for what it is.

An avoidance.

"Hey." Kade's hands, with their thick, callused palms cupping the tumbler of whiskey, encroached into my view. "You know I'm fucking with you, right? Where you go, we go. There was never a choice about that."

He's right.

And he's wrong.

That's what has guilt beating me like a prize fighter pummeling a boxer far past his prime. I can't even put up a defense, so I absorb the blows, arms stretched wide, chin tilted, ready for the swing that will lay me out and put me out of my misery.

Because in the last nine and a half years, wherever I've led, Kade, Mac, Gideon... They've all followed. Not blindly. They're all too proud, too intelligent and strong to follow anyone like sheep. It's loyalty that has kept them by my side even when I've been set on a countdown to my personal Armageddon.

Kade's also wrong. He had a choice just as the rest of them did. They could've decided to remain in L.A. instead of uprooting their whole lives and moving over a thousand miles to be with me and Gunner. The smart thing to do would've been to wait it out back in California, see if sobriety, fatherhood and this change in lifestyle stuck. Determine what kind of singer, musician, fucking *person* I am without the drugs.

That should've been their choice.

But no. They're here with me. Having bought homes just a couple of blocks away from me. Helping renovate my carriage house into a recording studio. Giving the nine-month-old son I didn't know existed until ninety days ago a family.

Yeah, they had choices.

And, though there are moments—like this one—when I believe they all bet on the wrong horse—I'm still damn glad they did.

Yep, that's me. Still fucking selfish to the core.

"You know, when you get in moods like this I really wish you'd chosen fucking as a coping mechanism instead of working out."

My head snaps up, and I stare at him lips parted in horror and...wonder. Because *the hell*?

"Did you really just let that shit come out of your mouth?"

He shrugs one big shoulder, his eyes narrowing the slightest bit, taking a small sip of the whiskey.

"I'm just saying. I wanna swing on you so bad right now, but with those freakishly big muscles you got going on, I'm only twenty-three percent sure you wouldn't lay my ass out. But pussy? I could beat the shit outta you *and* there could be a threesome in my future..." He shrugs again.

"You do hear yourself, right? How incredibly insensitive and fucked up to hell you sound?"

"Maybe. But what's the saying?" He tips his head to the side, and the dark blond bun at the back of his head slides to the side. "Ain't no fun if the homies can't have none."

I snort. And wonder if maybe sensitivity training for rock bands is a thing.

Shaking my head, I set my apple juice on the table and push to my feet. Stretching my arms above my head, I scan the living room, taking in the still unpacked boxes stacked against walls. I'd only brought things with me from L.A. that I absolutely couldn't leave behind, not wanting to drag any of that old shit with me to my fresh start in Pike's End. One of the most common triggers for relapses is being around the people, places and things that surrounded you while deep in your addiction. For Gunner's sake—and mine —I had to leave.

But I couldn't part from certain things. Like my guitar collection. My parents' wedding album. My mother's china set, passed down to her from her mother, that I took with me all those years ago when I left Pike's End, afraid Dad would destroy it in one of his drunken fits. My gran's afghans. And more items that someone like me shouldn't be sentimental about.

Lowering my arms, I roll my shoulders back. Tomorrow, I'll tackle the rest of it. Finish unpacking and attempt to hit reboot on this new life I insisted on. But for now, a restlessness crawls under my skin like a convoy of ants and I need to get moving.

Get out.

Just for a little while.

"I'm going for a run. You want to come with me? Matt's got Gunner down for the night and can listen out for him while we're gone," I say, mentioning our "manny" Matt Kramer, who moved with us to Pike's End.

Kade snorts.

"A day of driving, more hours of unpacking and a punishing run to top everything off. *Or* I could crash on your couch and cuddle up with this," he held up his glass, "for the night. Tough choice, but I'm choosing B."

Swinging his legs up and around, he propped his feet on the far arm of the couch and reclined on the other one. Bringing his drink to his mouth once more, he extended his arm for the remote on the table and aimed it at the television mounted on the wall. Because, of course, one of the first things we did was connect the eighty inch monstrosity.

Snorting, I jerk my chin up. "And you wonder why you can't take me."

"Twenty-three percent, muthafucka. I said a twenty-three percent chance."

I turn around, laughing under my breath when the sound of my name stops me. Pivoting, I face my best friend again.

"I might've been teasing earlier, and yeah, I probably took it too far. And you're my brother in every sense but biology, so trust that I recognize your addiction is a disease not to be made light of. And I admire the fuck out of you for staying sober. We all do. But I'm dead ass about you being so hard on yourself. You need to give yourself a break. And grace. You deserve it."

He switches his attention back to the TV and immediately becomes engrossed in an episode of *60 Days In*, acting as if he hasn't left a drummer's fist-sized hole in my chest.

Not that he's looking at me—not that I can speak —but I nod and head for the hallway and the stairs the lead to the second level of the old farmhouse. Within moments, I climb the steps and stride down the hall.

As I pass my son's doorway, my feet slow. A soft, golden glow spills from the cracked door, and I can't resist the pull. Not of the light, but the small human being whose presence levels my life, rendering everything but him unimportant and insignificant.

In moments, I cross the large room decorated in soft blues and yellows in a *Jack and the Beanstalk* motif. Once I bought the house, I had a local interior designer come in and ready the room so Gunner would spend his first night in his own crib with a mobile of beans, miniature Jacks and geese circling over him.

Quietly approaching the crib, I'm not even aware of holding my breath. Not until my lungs start to burn and scream for mercy. Only then do I release the pent up air, low and deliberately. I've had him for three months now. Eighty-seven days, to be exact, since his mother—a woman I'm ashamed to admit I can't remember since I was most likely lit when we fucked—dropped him off at my agent's office.

And in those nearly three months, there hasn't been one time that I've looked at him and my breath didn't catch in my throat.

Including now.

I stroke a hand down his soft, dark blond curls, my palm settling on his back, savoring the rise and fall signaling his steady breathing. I quietly smirk. At least I no longer put my finger under his nose. Underneath my hand, Gunner snuffles, squirming a little, then sticks his thumb in his mouth. I wait several moments for him to still, and then I lift my arm and back away from the crib, leaving my son to sleep on. Seeing him like that, so peaceful, I'm almost convinced everything will be okay.

And a half-hour later, as my feet pound the pavement and the late October night air whispers over my sweat dampened face, I try to hold on to the residue of that certainty.

But I might've miscalculated venturing out so soon. Even though the silence is disturbed by the occasional dog bark, the call of nocturnal insects and the random muffled voice behind the curtained, dimly lit windows, the memories crowd in on me, suffocate me.

The hood of my sweatshirt covers my bent head, and I stare down at the sidewalk, purposefully not staring at my surroundings. But I don't need to. I know where my feet took me without my conscious permission.

This is my hometown after all.

This is—what had Kade called it?—Bumfuck, Washington. Otherwise known as Pike's End. The place that had only ever seen me as John Sullivan, the town drunk's, delinquent son. Didn't matter that the worst crimes I'd ever committed were shoplifting out of Walden's Drug Store when I was twelve and a couple of speeding tickets years later. This town and its residents never really accepted me, but waited to see just how rotten and twisted I would turn out. I didn't feel wanted here. Wasn't happy here.

And yet, I'm back...here.

Rich beyond even my imagination. More fame than money. And still, I've proven every one of them right about me.

Tucking my chin, I deliberately blank my mind and focus on nothing but the stretch and pull of muscle. Drawing air in through the nose and pushing it out through my mouth. The sweet ache singing through my body. It all but drowns out the noise.

It almost smothers the sly, slick craving that slinks in the back of my brain. Sometimes, it's quiet. But at moments like these, when I'm on edge and doubts and emotions roil in my chest and head, it's a little bolder, greedier.

Gritting my teeth, I run on.

And next time I glance up, I have no idea how I ended up in Cedarbrook Park, standing by the edge of the creek that runs through the rear of the park. Have no idea, but I'm not shocked. A sort of...resignation weighs on my chest because this was inevitable. My mind might not have acknowledged the urge or permitted the need, but the raw, primal part of my subconscious? It overrode all of that and brought me to the place where me and Lennon used to meet in secret.

The place my heart had thrown itself to the ground to lie at her feet, a willing sacrifice.

The place I'd promised to love her forever, to never hurt her.

I pinch the bridge of my nose, my eyes closing. Air rushes in and out of my lungs, but not because of my run. Because I can no longer outrun myself, the memories. They bear down on me like a speeding car, and staring into the headlights, I freeze, can't move. Instead, memory after memory slams into me.

God.

My fists clench, my body damn shivering against the impact. I can even smell her. That scent of violets —sweet and earthy—with notes of a sensual musk weaving around it like a vine. That scent followed me into my dreams, into my waking hours for years, haunting me. Even now, standing here in this sacred place of ours, it's headier, more tangible...

Wait.

My heart attempts to drill a hole through my chest, and a rush of sound fills my head like a howling wind trapped in a cave. Though every sense of self-preservation screams that I leave, I don't heed it. Instead, I slowly turn and...

Fuck.

I blink. But no. She doesn't disappear into the dark mists of my mind like she has too many times to count over the last decade. She isn't a vision my fevered, hungry mind conjured. No, somehow she's here. She's real.

"Lennon."

If I possessed any lingering doubts that it was her standing in front of me, that slight flinch she couldn't quite manage to control swept them away.

"King. I'd heard you were back."

That voice. In my dreams, it had remained the same. And it is...but different. Huskier but with the same low, cultured tone that she'd perfected even at eighteen.

Sliding my hands in the front pocket of my hoodie to hide their sudden trembling, I jerk my chin. "That was quick. It's been what? Seven hours?"

"More than enough time to catalogue everything unloaded from your moving van, discuss exactly where you placed each piece in your house and speculate on whether or not you plan on turning Pike's End into a den of rock 'n' roll iniquity like L.A."

I snort and pretend the tightness in my chest is acid reflux from the Chinese food from dinner and not due to resentment.

"Small towns. I almost forgot that being in everybody's business was part of its charm."

"Why are you here, King?" she abruptly asks, voice hard.

As hard as that last email she sent me.

Fuck you for making me believe in you.

Fuck you for making me love you.

Every message, every word in them is branded in my brain, and I can recite them like a pastor quotes scripture. Since they're all I have left of her, they've become my gospel—life and damnation.

"Here in this park or in Pike's End?"

A beat of silence passes between us and it's as deafening and as long as one of Kade's drum solos. And as quiet and fleeting as a moment of true joy.

"Pike's End," she finally says.

"Coward," I murmur.

What the fuck am I doing? I knew at some point our paths would cross—it's inevitable in a town this size. But my plan had been to be polite, keep my distance, follow her lead. I'm in no position to push. But here I am...pushing.

"I see you haven't changed." Anger licks through her voice, and maybe I am a glutton for punishment because I shiver as if the hot tongue of it glides over my damp skin. "Still playing games." She steps forward, and the wind shifts the leaves on the tree limbs, moving the shadows as well. Like a stage curtain, they part over her face, exposing the slight sneer curling the corner of her mouth. "Still so careless and arrogant. You don't give a damn how you fuck up your life, so why should you care about how it blows back on other people's?"

I'm better than her at controlling my physical reactions. My years in the music industry taught me early on that emotions—revealing them, giving people access to them—are like throwing chum in shark infested seas. So, yeah, I'm a pro at regulating what I allow people to see. But inside? Inside, I'm reeling at her words and the sight of her face cast in sharp relief by the moonlight.

Her voice isn't the only thing about her that's the same but different.

At twenty-eight, the roundness of youth had disappeared, leaving a sharper, more refined bone structure behind. Cheekbones so high, so sharp a person could experience vertigo staring at them. A proud slope of a nose with wide, flared nostrils. A deceptively delicate jawline that I know from personal experience could turn stubborn in seconds. The faint dent in her chin that she'd loved because her mother used to tell her it was where God had kissed her.

And then there's her mouth.

A mouth that seems blasphemous to put in the same sentence with God. Because it's sin incarnate. Sin and sex and temptation. That full upper lip with its deep dip in the middle and the even fuller lower curve that... A shudder ripples through me as I stare at that lewd mouth, and I lock my muscles against it. Nothing, though, can prevent the hot bolt of lust jolting through me. Or stop the throbbing in my cock that echoes the drumming of my heart. I clench my fingers tight in my pocket in order not to splay my fingers wide over the out of control organ...and not to fist my dick in a punishing grip. And stroke it. Get myself off just at the sight of those lush, profane lips.

What would Lennon do?

Curse me for being even more of a thoughtless, egotistical asshole and leave?

Stand there and watch me with hate and arousal burning in those dark, bedroom eyes?

Or...

Come closer. Kneel down in front of me like she used to, tip her head back, part those beautiful lips and let me inside. Suck me down until my cock nudges the back of that tight throat before she breathes slowly, relaxes and lets me breach that tunnel...

Inhaling a deep breath, I take a step back. And then another. Because I can still feel the phantom caress of those rough silk, dark brown curls between my fingers and over my palm. And the vibration of her pleased hum down my dick.

Standing here in this place with her, the memories like a third, asphyxiating presence, it's a danger zone. Part of me is drawn to her like a lonely, shivering traveler craving the warmth of a fire in the dark. And the other part shakes in terror because that insatiable need, that hunger could send me spiraling. She could so easily become my next addition...or send me plunging headlong back into my old one.

"Nothing? No witty comeback? No smart-ass remark?" she demands, the corner of her mouth curling higher into a harder sneer.

"What do you want me to say?" I ask, smothering the urge to retreat until the shadows swallow me up. Until I disappear into the shame and guilt. "Defend myself? I'm not going to do that. There's no point. Should I beg for your forgiveness? As if I have a chance in hell of receiving that."

"Forgiveness?" She laughs, and there isn't shit humorous about it. The sound is caustic, corrosive. She tilts her head to the side. "That's for Bible stories and Christmas movies. You won't find that here. I. Hate. You."

Those last three words are bullets striking me dead center mass, and I almost press my palms to the injuries they've left behind.

But maybe it's a byproduct of living with a drunk. Some people learn to duck and hide, avoid confrontation and ugliness at all costs. I run at it, fists and chin raised. Even when I'm guaranteed to crawl back bruised and bloody.

And in this fight, that's the only way I'm coming out of it.

"Don't stop there, Lennon," I murmur. "It's been ten years. You can't tell me that's all that you have. Give me more, I can handle it."

"Give you more?" An almost imperceptible tremor quivers in her voice, and her rage heats the night air. And as sick as it might make me, I want to reclaim the space I inserted between us and bask in it. Because I'm desperate. So fucking desperate. And I'd rather have her hate than her apathy. She shakes her head, those thick curls grazing her shoulders, her jaw. "I don't give a damn about what you can or can't handle just like I don't need your permission to speak my mind. It's a little quirk I have."

Despite the pain using me for target practice, humor bubbles behind my sternum. Another thing that hadn't changed. Her tongue that could be sugary sweet and deadly sharp, even at eighteen. I'd enjoyed both edges of it.

"Lennon..."

"No." She throws up her hand, shoving it out towards me as if she can shove my words back at me just as easily. "I don't want to hear it. I don't want to hear anything from you, King. You don't get to be the victim here."

My stomach caves under the impact of that vocal blow.

She can't understand how I've struggled with that word—victim.

I decided to do my first line of coke. I let the music take a backseat to the indulgent, wild, selfish lifestyle that was all about me, my pleasure, my needs. Those were my choices, my decisions, and I own them. And those choices had direct and indirect effects on everyone around me—from my band, to the people we employed, to the label, to the fans. And definitely the music.

There also came a moment in the depths of my addiction when I couldn't stop. Something primal inside of me—the man who'd escaped his small, judgmental town with hope, stars and hunger for *more* in his heart—had cried out in pain. Begged that I put the drugs down. Walk away. Just say fucking no. As if it could be that simple. The truth is I willed myself into this addiction but I couldn't just will myself out of it. It had a hold on me—mentally, physically, emotionally. Addiction crept into and hid out in the dirty, unswept corners of my soul, the places where all of my fears, insecurities, anger and grief grew and spread like mold never revealed to the light. Yeah, I couldn't free myself of the monster's grasp. I had invited something in that overtook my life, and I became the slave to its master. And not until I opened the door and walked into rehab could I break the chains.

And even now...even free... There are times I hear the clanking of those chains, calling me. But now I lean on my family instead of the drugs to get me through the darker moments. Because I'm still a work in progress.

So am I a victim? No. I'm in a murky, complicated place in between.

There'd been a time when I could tell her all of this—or none of it. And she would still understand. Still get me when no one else truly had. But we're no longer those people to each other.

And I'm to blame.

"I should be used to your silence. You're good at that." She scoffs and starts to turn around. To leave.

The panic that wells up inside me, scratching and clawing at my gut, should be a red, blaring warning to slow down. To give us both space. Instead, I'm again rushing forward, plunging into the blast of her rage, gulping it down without thought or care that it might drown me.

"L.A. was a trigger." She halts mid-turn, the shadows and her hair concealing nearly everything but the outline of her nose and the curve of her mouth from me. She doesn't face me again, but she isn't walking away either, and taking that as a win, I continue. "I got...heavy into drugs." Fuck, it hurts revealing that to her of all people. Even if she already knows. And there's a good chance she does. Hell, she would've had to be living in a blackout zone not to hear about my epic, humiliating meltdown. Still, in this moment, I'm thankful for the darkness.

"When I came home from rehab, all the old places, people and temptations were still there. I stayed sober, but if I wanted to remain that way, I needed a change of environment. It's not the same for all ex-addicts. But for me, I couldn't" I shake my head.

Seeing the people who I'd snorted and smoked with, fucked ... Driving by the places I'd partied in, lost a part of my soul in... It'd all gotten to be too much. And some nights that tug had become damn near unbearable. Only the presence of Gunner in his room and either Kade, Mac or Gideon camped out in one of the guest rooms had kept me from crawling into that pit again.

"So I decided to move back here. I wasn't much wanted when I lived here before, but it was the safest place I could think of at the time. And Leif is here." I pause, consider my next words and whether to utter them or not. But my sobriety is about truth. And since there are already so many secrets between us—secrets I can never reveal—I won't allow this one, even if it would be by omission. Besides, in this town gossip is the second most popular religious denomination next to Baptist. It's not like it would remain private for long. "And then there's my son."

She doesn't say anything but her petite frame stiffens, her shoulders curling in the slightest bit.

"He's only nine months, but I needed to give him a safe space to grow up, surrounded by family and community. A place where everyone knowing your name or not being afraid to lock your doors at night isn't just a lyric in a song or a pretty myth. My childhood may not have been the best or the most stable, but he deserves it."

The silence thickens, dense and snarled with emotions that aren't so clearly identifiable as anger, sadness, scorn, pain. They're all of those. Maybe none of them. And they're emanating from Lennon in a mess so tangible I could reach out and pull on a tangled strand.

"His name?" she asks, and the low, hoarse question is so low, I almost miss it.

No, I don't. I couldn't miss one fucking thing about her, I'm that damn attuned to her.

"Gunner."

The overwhelming need to share every wondrous detail about my son propels the words to the back of my throat, to my tongue. I even open my mouth, but she turns her head and looks at me in the next moment. And the words curl in on themselves and die there.

Even the shadows can't hide the stark pain that glitters in her dark eyes. It drives the air from my lungs, and I damn near stumble back, away from that agony like the fucking coward I called her. But it's me who wants to run, to disappear. Because staring into those bottomless, beautiful eyes, I can't escape from the inescapable.

I caused the hurt turning her brown eyes nearly black.

I'm the reason for the hard edge of bitterness in this woman who'd been nothing but soft lines and curves.

Another thing I have to own.

"Lennon," I rasp.

"Welcome home, King," she whispers and turns

around, giving me her back. "Now stay the hell away from me."

With that parting shot, she walks away from me, and in seconds, she disappears and I stare at the spot where she stood. Only the faint scent of violets and musk and the dull pounding of my heart and cock assure me she was here.

And that I'm well and truly fucked.

3

Lennon

I need a moment.

Closing my eyes, I inhale and hold the deep breath, then seconds later, release it. And wait.

Oh yes. A smile curls my lips as satisfaction glides through me.

Blessed quiet.

Don't get me wrong. I love teaching the third grade. And I adore my students. Inquisitive, energetic, hilarious, super smart and terrifyingly blunt, they're a joy to greet and educate. Even on those days when they work my nerves like there's going to be a bonus check in their report cards. There's nothing else I'd rather be doing than teaching.

And yet... I savor the calm and quiet at the end of the day after they've all steamrolled down the hallway to their buses or car rides home.

"That right there is the face of someone who is giving thanks for 2:55 pm and the end-of-the-day bell." An evil chuckle follows the pronouncement, and I squint at Lena Graves, the elementary school's administrative assistant. "What happened? Daryl Rhodes tell you your breath stink again?"

I groan but ruin it with a loud snicker.

"You know he's ruined tuna fish for me, right? Like forever. I'm thinking about moving his desk next to Holly Turner. She had tuna *with onions* the other day for lunch. That'd show him."

Lena threw her head back with a loud cackle, her gorgeous, long dreads—died a deep blue this week—swing over her shoulder, revealing the other shaved side of her head.

"That is a whole level of petty, and I aspire to attain it." She grins, still laughing as she moves farther into my classroom.

I arch an eyebrow as she props a hip against one of the bookcases.

"Uh, aren't you supposed to be in the front office?"

"Nah, ol' girl is in there. Since she seems to know everything, she can hold it down while I get a cup of coffee." Lena holds up a white mug with the school's red and white logo on it.

I shake my head but can't contain my chuckle. "Ol' girl" is Tracey Morley, the new admin assistant hire. According to Lena, the younger woman barged in on her first day, "showing her ass" and trying to run things, and the two had been taking verbal swipes at each other ever since—a whole two weeks. Sometimes I wonder if they'll make it to week three without bloodshed.

"And you call *me* petty. There's a coffee pot right there in the office," I point out.

Lena shrugs a shoulder. "Must've forgot."

She didn't forget shit.

"So are you here biding your time until you have to return to the scene of the crime or did you drop by with a purpose?" I cross to the far side of the room and start straightening desks and picking up any stray pencils and papers left behind.

"Both," she says, grabbing a desk closest to her and mimics my actions, helping me out.

Which I'm grateful for. The sooner I clean up in here, the sooner I can head home and...hide.

God, I hate that my brain supplies that particular word to describe me turning off my phone, throwing a frozen pizza in the oven and curling up in my bedroom with wine, the remote and about three locked doors between me and the outside world.

I hate even more that the word is appropriate.

But that's what one glimpse, one conversation with King Sullivan has reduced me to. A shaken woman battling hermithood.

Giving myself a hard mental shake—and an even harder slap for letting my thoughts drift to *him* for the hundred-and-eleventh time *today*—I focus on the here and now. On Lena. Much less stressful and devastating. Much less dangerous.

"So," I clear my throat and slide the vocabulary test Miles left behind in his desk, "I get the first reason. What's up with the second?"

"I wondered if you heard King Sullivan is back town."

Her tone is casual, nonchalant but the simple statement seizes me in a crushing, implacable grip. My fingers clench around the edges of a desk, and it's a wonder the thing doesn't crumple like an accordion under my hold.

I stare down at it as if each grain of the wood on the desktop is worthy of careful inspection, so I don't have to glance over at my friend.

"Yes, I have heard," I say, careful to keep the chaos

roiling inside me at just the mention of his name out of my voice. "Dad mentioned it last night."

"Huh." A scrape of metal against laminate fills the room as Lena adjusts another desk. Then quiet. "How do you feel about it?"

Still refusing to look at her, I compel my body to move. To finish up this task so I can be free of this conversation I didn't ask for. These questions that are going to crack me right down the middle if they continue. After last night... After seeing him in the flesh... After hearing him speak about his son with such love...

"What're you talking about?" I force out a short laugh, but even to my ears it sounds too tight, serrated. Especially for someone who's only supposed to have a passing acquaintance with him. "How am I supposed to feel about it? I'm more of an Imagine Dragons girl than a Bloody Sunday fan."

"Really, Len? Is that what we're doing?" Lena quietly asked.

The use of my nickname and the solemn note in her voice has my head snapping up and my gaze crashes into hers. Concern darkens her hazel eyes, and I slowly straighten, a sinking feeling of dread bottoming out my stomach.

"I don't understand..." I haltingly begin, but she cuts me off with a slice of her hand through the air.

"I've been your best friend since the fifth grade. There isn't much about you that I don't know. Including" she cast a quick glance toward the open doorway and the empty hallway, then crosses over to the door and shuts it, "including the truth about you and King Sullivan," she concludes, retracing her steps but not stopping until she's sitting on a desk across from me.

Shock snags me by the throat, and I'm barely able to get out my ragged, "Lena..."

"Don't bother trying to deny it. You really believe you could keep anything from me?" She tsks as if I've disappointed her. And I don't know. Maybe I have. "Hell, it was me who dragged you to that party where you first met him. You couldn't keep your eyes off him. Then, after that night, you suddenly started disappearing. And Pike's End is only this big." She snapped her fingers. "I cut through the park one night on my way home from sneaking out and seeing Derrick. I saw the two of you," she murmurs.

"You never said anything," I say, astonishment still ricocheting through me.

"I almost did. But in the end, I decided against it. Len," she tilted her head, her hazel eyes both kind and piercing. "I hadn't seen you that happy in years. Not since your mom died. You hadn't said anything to me about King for a reason. And to keep that smile on your face and that joy in your eyes, I respected your decision. Even if I was worried that you would get hurt." She pauses, her gaze searching. "Which you did. And I'm assuming it's because he left."

"He promised to take me with him. We planned it." The confession pours out of me as if a rusty valve had been twisted deep inside me and the truth is gushing forward, unstoppable. Sinking down onto a desk, I let it all go. "After I graduated, we were going to leave for L.A. a week later, but he disappeared the night of graduation. I tried to contact him—we had to email because you remember how Dad was back then."

"Still is," Lena grumbles.

I huff out a short, dry laugh. "True. But since he monitored the phone bill, we couldn't risk it. And I would've done anything for him. I was ready to give up my only remaining family and the only home I'd ever known for him. I loved him that much. But I was nothing but a temporary diversion for him. Because as soon as he finished with me, he left Pike's End and I never heard from him again."

Until last night.

"Damn, Len," she breathes. "Why didn't you say anything? Let me be there for you? We could've driven down to L.A., hunted him down and busted out the windows on his car. Something."

I stare at her, then snicker. "While I appreciate the thought, a gross misdemeanor isn't necessary to express your love. And..." I shake my head, the murky, skeletal fingers of the past closing around my throat, and for a moment I almost choke on the memories. "And I was too humiliated to tell anyone. I felt stupid, foolish to have fallen for every one of his lines. God, he must've gotten such a kick out of how naïve and easy I was."

Disgust roils in my stomach at the thought of how I'd begged him to talk to me, pleaded with him not to leave me in those last emails. It's been years since I allowed myself to dwell on this; I'd shoved it into a dark, dusty drawer in my mind and refused to open it. Refused to revisit a time that had stripped me of my trust and faith in people.

I'd given King my virginity but it'd been his cruel deception and callous abandonment that had stripped me of my innocence.

"So I'll ask again, and no lies this time," she gently teases. "How're you doing with him being back in town?" Lena murmurs.

I heave a sigh and rub a hand over my hair, fingers bumping into the bun on top of my head.

"I don't know," I whisper. "Angry, which is a given. But also hurt, resentful...sad. The primary feeling, though? Fear? I'm so damn terrified."

"Of him? Or," she tilts her head, studies me, "of yourself?"

My lips part but my answer remains trapped in my throat.

I want to say, *I'm afraid of the changes his presence will bring to this town and, yes, to my life. King Sullivan has never left anything but chaos in his wake.*

But the half-truth tastes bitter and heavy on my tongue. Especially when, without the slightest nudge, my mind conjures an image of King from last night, standing by *our* creek in grey sweatpants that should've been illegal on his long, powerful thighs, and a thin, black hoodie that clung to his wide shoulders and chest like a thirsty groupie. Of course, I've seen pictures of him through the years. I can't live on planet Earth and avoid him or Bloody Sunday's music. Still, glancing at images of him and being within five feet of him is the difference between sitting in the dim, cool shade and bathing in the bright, hot sun. He's more vivid, bold, startlingly sexual...so real.

From the cheekbones that could've been chiseled from marble by a master sculptor's hand to the harshly carved line of his jaw that his short, full beard couldn't hide, and the almost cruel beauty of his mouth... From the deep, raspy sexiness of his voice that has sold millions and millions of records to the wild scent reminiscent of a violent storm and fresh rain... King was—*is*—a virtual experience that's immersive and overwhelming.

And I have zero plans of getting on that ride again.

That's just it, though. My head acknowledges that

keeping as much distance between us as possible is the best course. But my body is having the damnedest trouble getting on board that particular bandwagon. Last night... I briefly close my eyes, and without my permission, my mind waves a visual of King like the proverbial red flag. And right on cue, lust rushes through me, pinching my nipples tight, and I'm suddenly very thankful for the thick cable knit of my dress. It also conceals the instinctive clenching of my thighs against the bottoming out of my belly and the glide of heat pooling in a sweet ache deep inside my sex.

No, my body is definitely not with the "we don't want" program.

Good thing I control my vagina and the greedy, gullible hussy doesn't rule me.

And yet...

"I don't know," I quietly admit. "And that's the scary part."

Lena blew out a hard breath then stood and, taking a step forward, cups my hands between hers.

"Okay, babe, here's what we're going to do. Let's make a pact." She pops up two fingers, points them toward my face then back at herself. "You and me. Promise me, if you're about to do anything with, to, or regarding King Sullivan, call me first. Let me be your sounding board, and if need be, your alibi. Just keep me informed."

I choke on a burst of laughter that might be a little bit soggy from the emotion scratching at the back of my throat.

"What is your preoccupation with crime? Seriously, do I need to be worried?"

She shakes her head and gives me an earnest look. "Only a little. But a head's up? If the police come around asking about a bag of flaming dog shit on Ben's porch Monday night, I was with you, okay?"

"Holy shit." I gape at her. "Lena, you didn't."

"Of course not." She scoffs. "Plausible deniability is key here."

I groan. "Lena." It's so bad to laugh, and God knows I don't want to encourage her. But as I pull her into a hug, I can't contain my wide grin over her shoulder.

Because, as "ride-or-die" as Lena is for me, I'm just as loyal to her. And let's just say if her dick of a boyfriend was on fire and I had the only glass of water available, I'd drink it. Slowly.

A few weeks ago, Ben just up and left Lena, leaving only a Dear John letter, blaming her lack of motivation and ambition as his reasons for breaking up with her and going ghost. He, in the meantime, had absconded to Alaska to fulfill his dreams of crab fishing. You just can't make this shit up. And I work with eight-and-nine-year-olds with *very* creative imaginations.

It only took two weeks for Ben to show back up in Pike's End. And that includes travel days.

"Hey," I say, pulling back and cradling her shoulders. "Maybe we should make this a two way pact. If you ever feel like you might be on the verge of doing something, uh, unorthodox, call me first. That way you stay out of jail and I don't have to explain to the school board why my criminal behavior shouldn't prevent me from teaching impressionable young children." When Lena's eyes grow moist, I tug her back into my arms and hug her close. "And just my opinion? But girl. Ben—who couldn't commit to you or his so-called crab fishing dream— isn't worth having a record over. And you also know they don't have Netflix in jail. Now, Ben for damn sure ain't worth losing *that*."

A water-logged chuckle echoes in my ear, and guilt steals through me, leaving a slick, grimy path behind it. While I'd been so engrossed in breaking up with Justin, managing my dad's reaction and work, I'd missed that my friend was hurting—*is* hurting. Never again, though.

"So deal? We have a double pact?" I lean back and hold up a pinkie.

"Deal." She hooks hers around mine. "Thank you, Len."

"You don't need to thank me. This is what we do."

She smiles, then tilts her head. "But just to verify... Monday night. *Love and Hip Hop* and pizza. Y'know. Just in case."

I grin. "Got it."

4

King

"*Holy fuck*. It's an honest to God malt shop. I promise you; I've only seen one in Archie comics." Mac twists in the passenger seat, his wide, barrel chest straining against the seat belt. "We *have* to go in. If only just to see if Pop Tate is there."

I snicker as Gideon groans from the backseat.

"Careful, bruh. Your teenage girl is showing."

Mac doesn't turn from the window but he lifts an arm, his middle finger extended. "And she's loud and proud, muthafucka."

Gideon's low, rumble of a laugh rolled throughout the car, and I grin. Mac, Gideon, Kade and I—we're more like brothers than best friends and bandmates. And like any family, the members possess different personalities. Mac, the sensitive, playful one. Gideon, the more reserved, broody member. Kade, the extrovert big brother. And then there's me.

The fuck up.

And yet, here we all are. Back in my hometown where they all moved to be with me and my son.

I don't know where I would be without them.

And as I park across the street from Hunt Auto, I'm even more grateful for having them here with me.

Shutting off the engine, I stare at the garage where my brother has worked since he was eighteen. Right after I sacrificed everything to keep him out of jail for a ten year stretch.

Clenching my jaw, I jerk the keys out of the ignition and push open the car door. Immediately, a sharp whine and a cry of "Dada! Dada!" reaches me, and the shit filling my chest like a block of cement breaks apart. While shutting my door, I'm opening the back one, and I smile down at Gunner. As soon as he sees me, his beautiful scrunched up face clears into a smile that matches my own, exposing his two bottom teeth, and he lifts his chubby arms towards me. The pressure of too much emotion swells inside me, and my skin is almost too tight, too small to contain it. How is it possible for a twenty pound baby to wield so much power over me? To completely own me?

"If he didn't have me wrapped me around his finger, too, I would really roast your ass right here and now for that goofy look on your face," Gideon says.

I snort, releasing Gunner from his car seat and picking him up. His warm weight settles against my side, and he immediately starts babbling, patting my chest and glancing around. His thick, dark blond curls tickle my chin, and I rub a hand over them, the cool strands and his sweet non-stop "talking" a comfort as I stare up at the garage. The bay is open and several people work on cars that are either on the ground or on the hydraulic lifts. Hunt Auto took care of the usual tune-ups, alignments and engine work. But they were really known throughout the state for their restoration of older model cars. That's what Leif did and was damn good at.

"You good?" Mac claps a hand on my shoulder. Gideon bumps the other one.

"Yeah." Rubbing my chin over the top of Gunner's head, I repeat, softer this time, "Yeah."

Inhaling a deep breath, I cross the street, my friends flanking me. Instead of veering left to the office, I head for the bay. My heartbeat echoes in my head and my breathing is a loud whistling wind in my ears. I shouldn't be nervous about seeing my brother. I love him, and I'm so fucking proud of him. But there are the seeds of resentment, guilt and embarrassment that're wrapped around the love and pride. The seeds that have sprouted roots over the years and have grown an invisible but tangible barrier between us.

It's my fault, that barrier. So it's my responsibility to tear it down. I just wish I knew how.

Asa Hunt, owner of the garage, walks out of a side door leading into the bay, and he notices me first. He draws to an abrupt halt, eyes narrowing on me. I don't glance away from him—the motherfucker used to play football before he was injured but he's still huge —but I feel the other employees' eyes on us, hear their voices trail off.

Asa doesn't look away from me either even as he lifts his chin and shouts, "Leif. Someone here to see you."

Within seconds, my brother emerges from a back room, shutting the door behind him. Dressed in dark green overalls, he removes a pair of safety glasses and tugs a mask down.

"Yeah?" he asks just before the blue gaze we both share scans the garage and lands on me. Surprise flashes in his eyes, followed by a glimmer of happiness. But that dims quickly, and my little brother is unreadable. "King, I heard you were back in town."

No hint of accusation colors his voice but it's there. Or maybe that's my own guilty conscience supplying it. I didn't go by his house last night when I arrived in town. Didn't get a chance to call either. That's why I'm here. I just underestimated the speed of Pike's End's grapevine.

"Yeah, I wanted to come by and let you know." I glance over my shoulder as if I could peep the town gossips loitering on the curb across the street. "But it seems like the news already got to you first."

"There's this thing called a telephone," Leif says, voice conversational but with a flinty note. "And you didn't have to come to my job to see me, I have a home. Where we don't have an audience."

Yeah, that's not option. Leif has been out to visit me in L.A. over the years because I can't return to Pike's End. For...other reasons but also because of Dad. He's been gone three years now, but Leif still lives in the house we grew up in. I haven't been able to bring myself to return there yet. Too many memories. Painful ones. There's too much anger inside me, too much grief that I haven't resolved with Dad yet, which I'm still working on. I'd lost my mother, and he'd essentially taken my one remaining parent away from me by turning into an emotionally and mentally absent drunk. And then he died, taking away any chance for reconciliation or for me to air how I felt.

Yeah, I have issues.

"I can come back, Leif," I murmur.

He's quiet for a long moment, staring at me. But then his gaze drops to Gunner, and his eyes soften.

"Nah, you're here now. And so is my nephew." Slipping his glasses and mask over his head, he sets them on a counter and loosens his overalls, sliding them over his shoulders until they hang around his waist.

His black T-shirt hugs his lean frame as he moves toward us, giving chin lifts to Mac and Gideon before focusing all his attention on Gunner. "Can I?" he asks, holding his arms out.

"Yeah." I shift Gunner off my hip and into my brother's outstretched hands.

Gunner goes to his uncle without complaint, probably because he's a friendly baby, and Mac, Gideon and I are standing right there. He chatters away, his only really discernible word "hi."

Hearing it, Leif smiles and says, "Hi, Gunner. I'm your Uncle Leif."

My son smiles his gummy grin up at him, patting Leif on the chin, and I watch my brother fall in love with his nephew in real time.

"He looks like Mom," Leif murmurs, rubbing a hand over the baby's back as Gunner grabs his necklace and plays with it.

"Yeah, he does."

"Hey, Leif," Asa calls out. "Take the rest of the day off and spend with your family. That Chevelle can wait. We have another week before delivery."

Leif nods, his attention not wavering from Gunner, but Gideon holds up a hand, shifting forward.

"Hol' up. A Chevy Chevelle? What year?"

Asa arches an eyebrow. "A '64."

"Shit." He shakes his head, hazel eyes bright with interest. "Can I have a look?"

Did I mention he's the reticent brooder and a *complete* gearhead?

The corner of Asa's mouth quirks, and he shrugs a shoulder.

"Sure. What does the lead guitarist of Bloody Sunday know about cars, though?"

Gideon strides forward, oblivious to the wide, fascinated gazes that follow him.

"I was raised in a garage. My father and uncle were mechanics. They're coming up here from Baltimore for a visit. Don't be surprised if they drop in at your garage," he warned. Jerking his chin, he adds, "Hey, I have a '67 Chevy Camaro in storage back in L.A. If I have it shipped, would you do the work on it? Let me help out? I've always wanted to learn the restoration part of it."

Shit, this might be the most I've heard Gideon talk in one conversation.

Surprise flickers across Asa's face but he nods.

"Yeah, we'll take your business and your money." He smirks. "And having an honest-to-fuck rock star as an apprentice is good publicity." He tilts his head toward the rear of the shop. "Let me get you suited up and I'll take you back there to check out the Chevelle."

Gideon follows Asa, and Mac and I look at each other. He laughs while I shake my head.

"I guess that means we're staying a little longer," I drawl.

"I'm giving him ten minutes before I go back there and drag his ass out. We'll be here all night once he gets started," Mac mutters. "You," he jabs a finger at Leif, "go get your shit or do whatever you need to do. When we grab Gideon, we have to go. Fast."

"Understood." Chuckling, Leif turns, still holding Gunner. "I'll just go grab my"

"Hi, Leif. How're you doing?"

Shock reverberates through me, a ripple of pure ice that douses me, leaving me frozen. But a wave of heat pours through me like flame-lit gasoline, thawing the numbness. That's what just the sight of Lennon does to me. How just the sound of her voice impacts me.

If only it was as simple as my dick getting hard.

"Hey, Lennon," Leif greets my ex-girlfriend with a wide smile and a familiarity that has surprise and another, darker emotion churning in my veins.

Jealousy. Jealousy is that darker emotion.

And as Lennon moves closer to him, that sweater dress clinging to every flagrant curve of her tight body, it sinks its teeth into my flesh and bone, spilling poison.

Look at me. The demand growls inside my head. *Baby, look at me.*

If we didn't have so many eyes on us, I'd stalk over there right now, grab her chin, tip her head back and make her acknowledge me. Make her stare into my eyes and spit more of that hatred at me, more of that fire. I'd rather have that lick at me than have her ignore me.

Because she is ignoring me.

Lennon knows I'm standing here—the stiffness in her frame tells the story. The slight turn of her body as if dismissing me is the epilogue.

"Is that her?" Mac murmurs.

"Yeah, that's her."

Of course he's aware of Lennon. All of them are. Our past is one of the things that worried them about me moving back here. I left possible triggers back in L.A. But they feared my biggest one might've been waiting for me right here.

I fear the same thing.

And yet, she dominates my thoughts. My body transforms into a dangerous, snapping live wire at just the sight of her. The throb of my cock echoes in my pulse, my damn head.

My heart has a beat, a song that belongs only to her.

And I can't have her. Too many things stand between us like a fresh battalion of soldiers.

Her hatred of me.

My fear of fucking up and letting everyone down again. Including her. Including Gunner.

The decade-long secrets that still have the power to cut all of us—but especially Lennon—to the core.

"She's hot as fuck," Mac points out.

"Keep your opinion and your eyes to yourself," I mutter.

He chuckles and my next suggestion of how he can get cozy with his bass dries up on my tongue as Lennon reaches out toward Gunner and tickles his stomach. He giggles and clutches his belly, trapping her finger under his chubby fingers.

"Who is this adorable guy?" She smiles, tickling him again.

"This," Leif hikes Gunner a little higher on his hip, and grins, "is my nephew Gunner."

Her head jerks toward me, her dark brown gaze crashing into mine. Yeah, she knew I was standing here.

"Fuck," Mac whispers.

If I had breath, I would've echoed that.

Pain saturates her eyes, darkening them to a near black. I move forward—the need to ease that hurt from her instinctual—but Mac's hand gripping my forearm holds me back.

"Not your place, man," he says, voice low.

Logically, I know this. I do. But every cell in my body cries out that it's no one else's place, no one's *right* but mine. Even though I abdicated that right when I snuck out of this town like a thief, abandoning her.

She glances away from me, switching her attention back to Leif and Gunner. A strained smile replaces the more natural one she wore, but she still brushes the back of her finger along Gunner's cheek.

"Well, you're just beautiful, Gunner," she murmurs.

For a moment, that caricature of a smile drops and she dips her head. Jesus, my chest aches. My palms itch to rub them over her hair, her neck, back. To pull her close and let her rest her weight against me. Let me bear her up for however long she needs me. I want to be that person again for her. If I close my eyes, I can even feel her breath on the base of my throat, the press of her fingers on my skin. But I can't. And not just because she would never allow me to. I've hurt her once, and where I am, *who* I am—an ex-addict working to keep his sobriety, a new single dad learning every day what it means to be a father, a musician discovering what it means to work again, play again sober—would be a burden to her. A painful burden.

As the look on her face attests to.

"Lennon..." Leif says.

"Is Asa around?" she asks, cutting him off. "India said she talked to him earlier about me dropping my car off."

"He's in the back. I'll go get him for you." Leif glances over at me, and I'm there before he can call out my name.

"I got him."

Leif shifts a look from me to Lennon, the back to me, eyes narrowed. He hesitates, and it doesn't take a mentalist to read his body language. He's wary of leaving me with her.

He's not wrong.

Yet, I'm not moving away from her. No matter how much I'm courting our downfall.

"I'll be right back," Leif says, no, warns and turns Gunner back over to me.

"Lennon," I murmur. "How're you?"

She crosses her arms over her chest, takes a step back. "Fine." Her gaze falls on Gunner again, who's whining and wiggling in my arms. "This is your baby."

"Yes."

I catch her low, sharp inhalation seconds and, like last night, that almost imperceptible flinch she can't quite manage to hide.

"Len...*shit*."

With a squeal, Gunner launches himself out of my arms and straight toward Lennon. With a gasp, she catches him. My heart hurls for the back of my throat, lodging itself there, and she's shaking like a leaf, her arms closed around my son in a vise grip. Even Mac appears next to me, his breathing ragged. The only one unaffected by his acrobatics is Gunner. Babbling happily, he balls the front of her dress in one fist and bats at her earrings with her other hand.

"Oh God," she breathes, burying her face in his curls. "He scared the hell out of me."

"He must really like you." Mac laughs, and it's only a little bit winded. "Not that I can blame him."

At his words, she stiffens. Pain slashes across her face again, but unlike moments earlier, it doesn't smooth out. Her expression crumbles. And she gently untangles Gunner's fingers from her dress before carefully handing him to me.

"I need to go," she rasps.

Before I can object, she whirls around and disappears inside the side door leading back into the building.

"Take Gunner."

Mac accepts my son and sighs. "Dammit, King. This isn't a good idea."

No, it isn't. But that doesn't stop me from charging after her. The door opens into the garage's lobby and, ignoring the sudden silence and then loud whispers, I stalk across the floor, catching Lennon's arm just before she pushes open the door.

"King, what're you doing?" She jerks at my hold on her, but damn if I'm letting her leave like this. "The hell? People are staring," she hisses.

"Come with me then, and don't give them more to stare at or talk about." Turning to the front desk where a younger Black guy isn't even trying to pretend that he's not watching us, I tip my chin. "Where's your bathroom?"

"The staff's bathroom's through there." He jabs his thumb over his shoulder, indicating a closed door behind him. "Near the employee breakroom."

"Thanks." Not waiting, I slide my hand down her arm, grasping Lennon's hand and tugging her to the desk and around it.

I give it five minutes before the news of me dragging her through the lobby of Hunt Auto reaches most of the ears in Pike's End. This is what I wanted to avoid —becoming the subject of gossips over soda and meatloaf over at Rise 'n Shine Diner.

But I walked away from her once. Nothing could make me do it again while she wore her heart and pain etched into her face. Knowing I was the source of it again.

Fuck the gossip.

This isn't about me. It's only about her.

I bypass the bathroom, entering the breakroom instead and closing the door behind us. As soon as the lock engages, she whirls around, and I shift my gaze from her infuriated glare to over her head.

Just for a minute.

Because Jesus... She's fucking gorgeous.

My fingers itch to sink into those beautiful, thick curls, hold her steady while I desecrate that wide, lush mouth. The knit of her dress pays homage to every curve and dip of her body, molding to her high, firm breasts, the sensual flare of her hips, the thickness of her thighs. And fuck if I can't feel the heels of her knee-high boots in my lower back.

At twenty I'd barely had the opportunity to explore the searing sexuality and lust that had existed between us before I had to leave. Barely had my fill of that violets and musk scent that was more intoxicating than the best top-shelf alcohol, the fragrance that clung to the base of her neck and in the shadowed, moist valley between her breasts. Denser and richer in that tight, hot pussy.

My stomach aches with hunger for a woman whose particular flavor is still as fresh, as potent to me as it was ten years ago.

"What in the hell are you thinking?" she snapped, then flicks her gaze towards the closed door. She lowers her voice without losing any of the venom. "Do you know what you just did?"

"Yeah." I drag my gaze from the wall and meet hers. Not daring to glance below her chin. No, fuck that. Her nose. "I stopped you from driving while you were upset. And don't try lying to me," I interrupt when her lips part to do just that—lie. "You were upset. Still are."

"And if I am?" She turns her head away from me. "That isn't any business of yours. Anything regarding me stopped being your concern a long time ago. You made that decision for both us when you left."

Yeah, the blow of her words shudders through me, and I lock my muscles absorbing the impact. The clever motherfucker who said the truth hurts clearly possessed the gift of understatement.

"Don't ask me to see you hurting and walk away, whether it's my business or not. Don't ask me to do it."

"Why not?" She jerks her gaze back to me, and I go solid. "You do it so well. You're a pro at it."

I stare at her. At the tautness of the skin over her cheekbones. The darkness in her eyes. The slight tremble of her lips. And that same shiver ripples through her body. She's a bomb set on emotional detonate, and the masochist that I am, I want all that shrapnel embedded in my skin. I want her to draw my blood.

"Don't stop now," I push her like I did last night at the park. "Let it out, baby. You're right. I left you. Didn't look back. Didn't give a fuck." I lie.

"You don't give a fuck about anyone but yourself. You never did. You used me and then threw me away," she rasps.

"Yeah, I did. Now what?" I keep shoving at her, even though guilt slides through me like filth. "You want me to apologize? To crawl on my knees and grovel? To beg?"

"Yes." Her whisper echoes in the room as if she shouted it. "I want to see you hurt, sorry, suffering. Just like when you left me broken. You didn't give a damn then so don't pretend you do now. Nothing about you has changed, King. Not one fucking thing. And I hate you for it. I hate you for not once looking back at the wreckage you left behind you. I hate you for going on with life and living it like I never mattered while I had to face reminders and memories of you every time I walked out my front door. I hate you..." Her voice hoarsened, and she crossed her arms over her chest, bowing her head. "I hate you because you gave another woman what you promised me. A family. Gunner could've been ours. Should've been ours. But you stole one more dream from me."

Fuck.

Fuck.

It doesn't occur to me *not* to touch her.

Eliminating the space between us, I pull her into my arms.

"King, don't..." Her whisper ends on a sob, and I tighten my hold on her, pressing my lips to her hair.

"No. I can't. There's no way in fuck I can let you go right now." I inhale her, take her so deep into my lungs, her scent burns me, marks me. Rubbing my mouth over her hair, the edge of her ear, I beg, just like she wanted me to. "Let go, Len. Let go and allow me to be the one who carries you through it. Lean on me, baby. Just for a little while."

Her fists ball into my shirt, stretching the material at my waist. She rolls her forehead against my chest, and her jagged breaths scorch me through my clothes. I slide a hand up her spine, cupping the back of her neck, squeezing it.

As if that unlocks something inside her, her shoulders shake and seconds later, her cries rip through the room. She crushes her cheek against me, and her tears dampen my shirt and skin. Stroking her back with one hand, I cradle her head with the other, fingers tunneling under the bun to scratch her scalp.

How long she sobs in my arms, I'm not certain.

Minutes, hours. A lifetime. It's not long enough. Closing my eyes, I soak in the feel of her. Her breasts a firm weight pressed against my abs. Her thighs riding one of mine. Her soft belly cradling my dick.

Curling my body over her, I brush my mouth over her ear.

"I left, yes. But I did look back. So many damn times. And never, ever did I stop giving a fuck," I softly admit.

Her breath shudders against my chest, and locking down a groan, I lift my hands to her face, tilting it back. Her eyes, moist with all the tears she's shed, meet mine. Even with her face wet and swollen, she's beautiful to me.

"Liar," she accuses, voice so rough, it's nearly painful to hear. "You're such a fucking liar."

Then she raises on her toes and crushes her mouth to mine.

Shit.

Shock seizes me by the back of the neck, shakes me like a rag doll. And I'm so caught in its ruthless grip that I can't move. Can't respond. Just feel the soft yet firm give of her full lips as they part over mine. Just receive the electrical charge of lust that pulses through me in wave after wave.

But that paralysis doesn't last long.

In seconds, a groan rolls out of me, and I open my mouth wider, thrusting my tongue deep. *Oh fuck, the taste of her.* It's richer, headier than the memories my dreams supplied. My hands shift from her cheeks up to her head, and damn, how I wish her hair was down so I could dig my fingers into those thick, coarse curls. Lose another part of myself in her. For now, I grab her bun, tug on it and tilt her head farther back, granting me even more access to this dick tease of a mouth.

And I take it.

I take it all.

Like a desperate, starved man, I feast on her, sucking, licking, biting. I'm a sinner, and gluttony is my crime but I'll willingly sign up for hell. And maybe Lennon craves the idea of being my downfall because she angles her head and proceeds to fuck my mouth and mind. I thought I'd wrestled control of this kiss away, but she's amending that misconception. With every lap at the roof of my mouth, each tangle and twist of her tongue around mine, each graze of her teeth over the tender flesh inside my bottom lip, she's owning me.

And I willingly submit.

Lowering an arm, I cup her hip, reacquainting myself with the sexy curve. I pull her closer, grinding my cock into her belly, seeking some kind of relief but only receiving a harder dick.

I'm doused in delicious heat...and then I'm shivering in the cold.

Lennon tears away from me, moving back until several feet separate us.

The serrated sound of our harsh breathing punches the air. We stare at each other like two hungry yet wary predators facing off. I draw my bottom lip between my teeth, running my tongue over it. Savoring the taste of her.

Lennon's eyes narrow on my mouth, and it's low, damn near indiscernible, but I catch it. That small, muted whimper. It's needy, unsatisfied. And it wraps around my cock like her delicate but strong hand, pumping my flesh.

Goddamn. Kissing her was the biggest mistake I made.

Fuck, I want to make it again.

"I shouldn't have done that," she whispers, echoing my thoughts. "*We* shouldn't have done that."

"If I apologize I'd be the liar you called me."

I am a liar, and a shitload of other things. But not about this. I don't regret putting my mouth on her again.

"You have an answer for everything, don't you, King?" She shakes her head. "For everything except the one thing I've wanted to know for the last ten years." Her shoulders stiffen, draw back, as if she's bracing herself against a body blow. "What happened? Why did you leave? Why did you change your mind about... Why did you change your mind?"

I stare at her, not blinking. The desire coursing through my veins ices over, a soul deep fear spreading like frost and snuffing out everything but the wild crash of my heart against my rib cage. Acid spills onto my tongue, and I try to swallow, but that would require my throat to work, and like the rest of my body, it's ceased all operation.

Tell her the truth.

The crazy idea sidles through my head, and for an even crazier moment, I latch onto it. Consider it.

I had to choose between you and my brother's future. Leif got popped for an auto theft charge because of a stupid joy ride, and your father threatened to send him away for ten years if I didn't leave town. Leave you. And if I tried to contact you in any way or tell you about his blatant abuse of power, he'd revoke Leif's parole and throw him in prison. I'd lost my mother, and for all intents and purposes, my father, too. My brother is all I had left, and I couldn't ruin his future. I couldn't sacrifice my brother's life for my happiness.

The words hovered on my tongue, screaming to finally be voiced.

But, I didn't say them.

Because, in the end, the truth would only hurt her, not free her.

Leif's parole had ended, and Terrance Ward's threats no longer wielded any power over us. But he would always be her father, the only parent she had left. That was one of the things that had bonded us. Pain over losing our mothers. It was a fucked up club no one wants to belong to. And while my father had become emotionally absent and an alcoholic, hers had tightened his grip, turning overprotective, nearly suffocating in his need to encase his only daughter in bubble wrap. It'd frustrated Lennon, even pissed her off at times, but she'd recognized the source of his need to shelter her. And she loves him.

I refuse to be the person who destroys her relationship with her father. I refuse to take away the one constant that's always been in her life.

I, for damn sure, haven't been.

So, even though this secret hangs around my neck like an albatross, I'll keep it.

Which means lying to her.

"We were too young to take off together. It was a nice dream but an unrealistic one. College, a home, a stable job—that was all in your future. Not living in a car or working in dive bars."

"That's bullshit." Her flat statement falls between us like a stone in a placid lake, the accusation behind it rippling out. "I don't know if you became a liar after you left here or if you were one all along. I'm leaning towards option B."

"Lennon…" But hell, I have nothing to say. I can't defend myself. The only defense against that is the truth—the one thing I can't give her.

"A part of me thinks you get off on this." She lifts

her arms as if to cross them over her chest, but at the last second, lowers them to her sides. I get it. After crying in my arms, after kissing me and betraying the need that still flares greedy and hot between us, she doesn't want to reveal any more vulnerability in front of me. Yeah. She has no idea how well I get it. "What? You don't have enough people throwing themselves at you, worshipping you, begging for you to notice them? Or for your..." Her mouth curls at the corner as her gaze drops to my still hard cock. "Attention? They're not enough? You also need the naïve girl stupid enough to believe in your bullshit?" She looses a harsh laugh. "Not that I haven't made it easy for you."

"Baby, that's not"

She slices a hand through the air.

"Don't call me that," she snaps. Then lower but fiercer, harder. "You don't get to call me that ever again."

Exhaling, she closes her eyes, and when she lifts her lashes, the steely resolve there has my stomach bottoming out.

Say something. Do something, goddammit. Don't let her walk out of here again.

But when Lennon gives me one last flinty stare, stalks around me and exits the breakroom, I say nothing. I do nothing.

Growing up the son of a drunk, teaches you to lie early on. Not just to other people but to yourself.

Dad's not feeling well. He'll stop drinking this time. You'll never see him in this bar again.

Years later, I'm still deceiving others. Still convincing myself I'm not a coward.

Still fucking lying.

Some things really don't ever change.

5

Lennon

There's an old saying that trouble comes in threes.

First, King Sullivan returns to town.

Second, I fall apart in front of him and then kiss him.

And now three. Dad and Justin descending the courthouse steps and heading toward me, wearing twin expressions of concern and determination.

I've never been one to buy into omens, but this? It has me checking out trees for a raven cawing "Nevermore."

Maybe I could—

Yeah, running or walking away in the other direction at a fast clip isn't going to work. I've managed to avoid Dad for the last two days, but eventually my luck would've run out. Tomorrow's Sunday, which means Sunday dinner. So maybe it is better to get this over with sooner. Because I have zero doubts this conversation is going to be about King and what happened at Hunt Auto. Still, on the courthouse steps? And with Justin, too?

Just...damn.

Swallowing a sigh, I paste a smile on my face and stop on the sidewalk at the bottom of the steps. It's not lost on me that I feel like a defendant waiting on a verdict from the jury. And judgment is striding towards me in three-piece suits and matching frowns.

"Dad. Justin." I turn up the wattage on my smile. "It's Saturday. In case you haven't heard, the courthouse is closed."

"The wheels of justice don't limit themselves to nine to five, Monday through Friday," Dad says, and that's not pretentious *at all.* "Justin asked for my advice on a case he's working on."

"Isn't that a conflict of interest? Especially if that case winds up in front of you?" I'm teasing. But...I'm not.

Dad already played the role of mentor to Justin before we started dating. But in the four years we were together, the lines between friends and jurist/attorney seemed to blur a little. Dad's favoritism towards Justin is the courthouse's worst kept secret.

"Don't worry, Lennon. Everything is above board," Justin informs me with a small chuckle. "Thank you for being concerned about me, though."

For the love of...

"Actually, I think my concern was more for the sanctity of the judicial system." I add a smile to it, but he had better read the room.

If he believes I'll cave to any pressure, subtle or overt, to give him another chance just because we're in front of my father, he really didn't learn anything about me in the last four years.

Could be he receives my message since slashes of scarlet darken his cheekbones and his lips firm into a flat line.

"I've invited Justin to lunch. Join us," Dad demands, because it's not an invitation.

"I'm actually on my way to meet Lena and India for lunch." I glance down at my cell phone's screen. "And I have about twenty minutes before I need to be there."

"Cancel. You work with them every day. They should understand that you're spending time with your father." Dad doesn't wait for my acquiescence, but starts walking off toward the courthouse parking lot, Justin beside him. "Follow us to the house."

"Sorry, Dad, but no."

He draws up short, slowly pivots and stares at me as if he doesn't understand the words I've uttered. That's fair. People don't usually tell the Honorable Terrance Ward "no."

"Excuse me."

I can't lie. My heart speeds up the tiniest bit and the muscles in my belly quiver. What daughter enjoys disappointing her father or witnessing that disapproval on his face? Not me. But I also can't allow his needs and expectations to supersede my own. I'm not his little girl anymore or someone appearing before him in his courtroom. Sometimes, he can't discern the difference.

"I'm sure Lena and India would understand if I asked for a rain check. But I don't want to. I've had plans for this all week. And being surrounded by children and co-workers all day isn't the same as a relaxing lunch for three. And the fact is, Dad," I glance at Justin, "this isn't just a lunch with my father. So, again, I'm sorry. But I have to request the rain check from you."

"Is this what you really want to do, Lennon?" he quietly asks.

"Decline a lunch invitation when I'll see you to-morrow for Sunday dinner? Yes, Dad, I'm comfortable making that decision," I reply in the same low tone.

He studies me, his gaze resembling brown chips of ice. A tiny muscle jumps along his clenched jaw. We both know we aren't talking about a simple meal.

"Maybe we should take this to my office," Justin offers, scanning the sidewalk and surrounding area.

Oh yes, can't have anyone reporting back that the judge engaged in a public spat with his daughter. Then they might start questioning the reason.

"Not necessary." Dad waves a hand, but he doesn't shift his attention away from me. "It seems my daughter isn't adverse to making a spectacle of herself lately, so this shouldn't be too uncomfortable."

The damage a boxer could wreak with his fists was nothing compared to the wounds my father can inflict with his words. And he had no problem laying people out with it—including me.

"If you want to talk to me about something in particular, then we can do that. But I'm not going to stand here and trade innuendoes or have you jab at me, Dad. I don't deserve it."

"When I see you making mistakes that will jeopardize your future then, as your father, I have the right to give my opinion." He tilts his head. "If you're making your decision, then, as your father, I'm going to make mine."

Foreboding trips down my spine, and a prickling dances over my scalp. I'm not accusing my father of issuing a threat, but that last statement felt...ominous.

"I'm going to be late for lunch if I don't leave now. I'll see you tomorrow for dinner," I say.

"Let's forego dinner tomorrow. Give one another space. We both have some thinking to do."

Pain flares inside me, bright and searing. I blink against the sting of tears but refuse to let any fall. I've met my quota of crying in front of men who have their own agendas and priorities when I'm not one of them.

Clearing my throat, I nod. "If that's what you'd like. I'll give you a call in a few days then." I glance at Justin one last time. "Justin."

"Lennon" He takes a step toward me, his arm outstretched towards me. "Let me walk you to your car or wherever you're headed. We have some things to discuss"

"No, I'm good." At this moment, with my heart an emotional punching bag, I can't handle another round of Justin's "We Belong Together" talk. I...can't. "And I don't want to interrupt your plans. See you later."

Not granting him the opportunity to object, I spin on my heel and walk off, not paying attention to where I'm going. Doesn't matter. I just need to get away from the suffocating weight of my father's disapproval.

Good luck since that would require somehow escaping myself.

WELL, DAD ENDED UP GETTING HIS WAY.

Huddling inside my coat, I stare at the majestic view of Mt. Rainier in the far distance. Through the dense border of trees, Puget Sound sparkles blue where the late October sun hits it. Boats of all sizes bob on the water, some far from shore and others docked out in our harbor. This peaceful, beautiful sight is the reason I come to this spot at the far edge of town. A tiny clearing surrounded on three sides by forest, it has one access road in, and I have to climb the small rise to reach this place. I found this slice of heaven by accident about five years ago while out driving, not expecting one of the several roads to bring me here. To what's become my haven. Here, it's just me, space and my thoughts. Or if I want, I don't even need to have those.

Like today.

Sighing, I ignore the cold and sink down onto the ground. Lena and India hadn't been angry when I bailed on our lunch date, but their concern had been evident. Especially Lena. I'd already violated our pact once with that trip into What-the-Hell-ville with King at Hunt Auto. But she didn't have to worry. Up here, no one could reach me. Not my father. Not Justin. Not the gossip.

Not King.

"What're you doing here?"

I bark out a sharp crack of incredulous laughter. And curse my body for perking up like, well, *anyone*, scenting bacon.

Isn't he my personal bacon, though?

Tempting, fucking delicious and bad for my health.

Tilting my head back, I pretend my vagina didn't just clench so hard I'll have interesting bruising there in a few hours and look into the unholy beauty that is King Sullivan's face.

"I'm minding my business. What are you doing here? Stalking is not only creepy, it's a crime."

His only reaction to my sarcasm is an arch of an eyebrow. But his eyes? I could get a sunburn from the intensity of that blue gaze on me.

"I own this property. Which means, technically, you're trespassing."

Frowning, I shove to my feet, dusting my palms on my black jeans. For a second, his scrutiny drops and lingers on my thighs, and *damn*. It's as if his long, elegant fingered hand palmed my legs, spread them wide and held me open for him to stare his fill.

My clit pulses behind my zipper and I'm dampening my panties with. One. Look.

"Since when?" I ask, covering my inconvenient lust with attitude.

I'm fighting for my pride and sanity here.

His gaze returns to mine. "Since I bought the house at the bottom of the hill." He jerks his head in the direction of a break in the tree line. "One of the conditions of the sale was the purchase of this land and the access road for privacy reasons. I didn't want reporters eventually finding their way up here to get pictures of not just me and the band but Gunner. My goal in bringing him here was for him to grow up as normal as possible. Every one of his moves being hawked and photographed and ending up on some tabloid site isn't my definition of normal." He twists and peers behind him as if he can glimpse the house and his son through the thick line of trees. "I should've taken care of finalizing all of the security details before we left L.A., but I thought I had more time."

"In my defense, I've been coming up here a few years now. I didn't know there was a house down there or that you'd bought it."

He turns back around and pins me with those bright, intense eyes.

"Did I say you needed a defense? Or accuse you of anything?"

"If I recall, your first words to me were, 'What're you doing here?'" I point out. "Sounds pretty accusatory to me."

He crosses his arms and the black leather jacket

and grey hoodie underneath pull tight over his wide shoulders and arms.

Stop looking at me like that. I swallow the demand but it sounds too desperate, too...revealing, even in my own head.

"No, it was 'what're you doing here?' as in 'are you okay?' because you're sitting alone in the middle of a forest. But," his chin tucks in toward his neck and once more that too-incisive perusal holds me in place as surely as a hand to the back of the neck, "it seems like you're spoiling for a fight. Is that what this is, Lennon?" He cocks his head, a gleam entering his gaze. "You want to get down and dirty, work out some of that anger and other shit that has you climbing hills and hiding out from the world?" He smiles, and *holy shit*. It's not nice. It's an invitation, pure and simple. Well, not pure. It's filthy and sinful. "Well, come on then. I'll let you dig your claws into me, kitten. I'll be your personal little scratching post."

And then he adds a crook of his fingers.

My breath turns to smoke.

Not surprising since liquid fire replaces the blood in my body.

My heart slows, and in between beats, I'm hyper-aware of every sensation, in tune with every sense. The sharp yet sweet scent of pine and fresh air with a note of rain. My own thunderous pulse in my ears and the echo of the air pushing in and out of my lungs. The sizzle and heat of desire snapping and lurching beneath my skin, softening my sex even as it's tightening my skin, my nipples, my belly. The tangy, biting flavor of excitement and fear on my tongue.

The startling blue of eyes that rival the Sound. The tangle of long, dirty blond hair carelessly pulled back into a bun with strands caressing his cheekbones, as if they, too, can't stand not touching him for long periods of time.

And God, my fingers tingle with the need, the primal *need* to just touch him.

I didn't come up here for this.

On the contrary, I sought this place of comfort to avoid the emotional mess in my life. Things have become so...complicated. And he's part of those complications. Him and the snarled, complicated chaos he triggers within me.

King's lying to me.

I know that as clearly as my own name.

And if there's one thing I can't abide, it's a liar.

Yet, standing here, with his challenge thrown down at my feet like a gauntlet, I don't care.

I don't care about anything but releasing all the rage, the confusion, the bitterness, the fucking hurt. And releasing it all on him.

He deserves it.

He should own it.

And he's safe enough for you to let loose on without harm.

Oh shut the hell up.

Yes, I'm arguing with myself, but honestly, there's no place for sentimentality here. Just unadulterated lust and animal instinct.

I stalk forward, shutting down reason and allowing desire to rule me. Here's where I should dig out my phone and dial Lena, but I don't want caution and logic.

No, I need to get lost in the madness, in the noise.

I need to get lost in King.

Not stopping until the tips of my boots bump his, I tilt my head back. He doesn't move, only watches me with hooded eyes. His beautiful, hard mouth carries a hint of a smirk, and I resent it even as my mouth waters with the desire to sink my teeth into the curve of it.

Slowly, I sink to my knees.

Shock flashes in his gaze, briefly widening it. Then lust darkens his eyes to cobalt and his skin tautens, throwing his chiseled facial features into sharper relief. Except his mouth. Those full, carnal lips appear more lush, more hedonistic. If the devil bears this face, no wonder the world brims with so many sinners.

"If you're waiting for me to say you don't have to or something like that bullshit, let me give you a heads up. It's not coming." He threads his fingers through my hair, gently at first, then firmer, scraping his blunt nails over my scalp. He twists his hands in my curls, tugging until tiny pinpricks scatter, making their presence known. My lashes flutter at the pleasure/pain sensation, reveling in it. "I want your mouth on my dick too much to ever be that much of a hypocrite. And I figure since you got on your knees, who am I to take your choice away?"

"Really progressive of you," I murmur, sliding two fingers underneath the hem of his hoodie and skimming the band of his jeans.

His stomach goes concave when my fingers skim his skin, and my own belly tightens in response, twisting and knotting.

"Progressive?" He grunts, half chuckles. "You must not have been listening." Then he covers my hand with his, stopping me from unbuttoning his jeans. He pinches my chin, tipping my head back with the other. "I meant what I said, Lennon. Take it out on me. I can handle it. But I draw the line at you coming out on the other side of this harmed."

"That sounds awfully close to 'you don't have to do this.'" I jerk my chin out of his hold, irritated.

Irritated that he's still talking when all I want from him are his pleas and groans.

Irritated that my heart fluttered at his concern.

"No, it's more 'make sure this is what you want.'"

Jerking his zipper down, I reach into his jeans and palm his heavy, thick cock. Because rock star. No underwear. So cliché. And one I appreciate.

Not wasting any time, I squeeze him, arrowing his long length down and into my mouth. Without preamble, I suck him. Pull him in deep. What started as a desperate move to shut him up backfires. At the first touch of his silk-over-steel flesh on my tongue, I'm gone. A moan rumbles up out of me at the salty, humid taste of him. Relaxing my jaw, I take more of him inside, sliding him over my tongue, lowering my head until that fat head bumps the back of my throat. Only then do I slowly withdraw, losing him with a small pop.

"Does that feel like I'm unsure of what I want?" I ask, lust roughening my voice to the consistency of gravel.

His eyes blaze down at me, and his hands knot in my hair, tugging. But I shake my hair, lifting my arms. Gripping his wrists, I pull on him until he untangles his fingers from my curls and allows me to clasp his hands together behind his back. Moisture trickles from my pussy to my panties, soaking them. Not just at my power play but at the knowledge that he's permitting me to have this control over him. We both know he can wrest it away, hold my head right where he wants it and fuck my face until he pours down my throat. He's done it before. Gentle and tender, but he's done it. But now, he's giving me this. The illusion of control.

And it's intoxicating.

Hooking my fingers in the sides of his jeans, I haul them down just a little more until the tops of his hips and that devastating V are visible. It'd take a stronger woman than me to resist the call of that tempting letter, and I've proven time and time again that when it comes to this man, I'm weak. I lean forward, dragging my tongue up one side of it, nipping his hip bone, then blessing the other side with the same treatment. It's worshipping beauty in the rawest manner possible. How it should be. With all that we are.

His big body trembles with the strain. To not grab me? To not take me to the ground? To not force me to take his dick back in my mouth?

I choose not to make him wait for that last one. Only because I don't want to wait.

Because that's why we're doing this after all. For me. For my pleasure.

Yeah, keep telling yourself that.

I ignore the smart-ass voice in my head and return my attention to the beautiful cock insolently nudging my cheek. Closing my eyes, I inhale his heady scent, redolent of rain clouds struck by lightning and fresh rain. It's more condensed here, so concentrated I could lick it off his cock, dip my head and sip it off his balls. Get drunk off it.

Is it any wonder I became enthralled with this man?

Parting my lips once more, I take him inside. His thighs bunch against my breast as his growl reverberates above me. I grip his hips for purchase and bob my head over him, sucking hard and slow. Then short and shallow. Flicking my tongue over the wide, plum shaped head, teasing pre-cum from the slit at the crown. Playing with the ridge under the tip. And King takes it all. His grunts and groans pepper the air, falling on me like gifts, each and every one of them.

And still, he keeps his hands behind him, giving me this. Being my—how had he put it?—scratching post.

I could toy with him for hours, that's how good he tastes, how addictive he is. But a fine tremble has taken hold of his body, and it's constant, as if there's an internal war waging within him and it's shaking him from the inside out. That same fire has taken ahold of me and my clit throbs while an emptiness yawns wide and deep inside my sex. I ache. It's edging close to painful, and one rub over my pussy would alleviate it, but that would mean letting go of King. And *that* I'm not willing to do yet.

Raising on my knees, I sink down on his dick. Sinking. Sinking. Sinking. Until, again, the smooth, big tip nudges the tight channel of my throat. But this time, I don't pull back. I push forward. I gag. And push forward, breath through my nose and deliberately relax my throat muscles. And push forward.

"Fuck, baby." Fingers grip my hair, disappear. "Goddamn, sorry." King's ragged breaths punch the air like torn up fists. "Baby, please, again. Again," he begs, demands. Somewhere in between.

Once more, because I want to, I slide off his cock but immediately return, sucking him down over and over. Tears stream from my eyes, but I don't care. I don't stop. Not when his hips thrust forward riding my mouth as more pleas fall from that dirty mouth. Pleas to "give him all of that throat," to "open wider and suck harder," and my personal favorite praise, "my baby loves to have her face fucked."

I shouldn't love that. But damn, I do.

My jaw aches, my eyes burn and my throat is sore, but still I slip him inside. And when his cock swells, filling me until I don't think I can take anymore, I do. And when he growls a warning, I don't pull back, I clutch his hips tighter, holding him closer and swallow every last drop of his cum, my name a roar in my ears.

And when he sinks down to his knees in front of me, scattering kisses over my eyes, cheeks and mouth, I sweep my tongue inside, granting him a taste of himself. And I almost orgasm when he sucks the residue of his release off my tongue.

Shooting to my feet, I toe my boots off and yank off one pant leg. Same with the panties. In seconds, I'm back down on the ground straddling King. He stares up at me, fisting his still hard dick, stroking it in a hard pump that looks a little merciless. I'm fascinated by his ministrations, and for a moment, I'm distracted from the lust tearing through me in a wild, destructive storm.

He's so fucking *beautiful*.

Just like that storm inside of me, he's the wind, the quake, the fire—complete beauty in chaos. He has the power to reshape, to create...and to destroy. I've seen his ability to destroy, been on the receiving end of it. And I'm so terrified to find out what we could look like reshaped from brokenness. What we could create from the ashes.

I shake my head. Luckily, I don't have to answer that question.

Flattening my palms on either side of his head, I lower my mouth to his until our breath mingles, mates.

"I don't have a condom on me," King quietly says.

"I can't and won't lie to you, Lennon. I've been with a lot of women, and a good number of them when I was fucked up on drugs. But I've been celibate since I've been in rehab. Six months. I was tested for everything in rehab and again when I got out. I'm clean. Still..." His gaze shift away from me, but not before I glimpse a hint of...something in them. Something that smacks too close to shame. "I understand if you don't want to chance being with me raw. I get it. And shit, I wouldn't advise it. C'mon." He lifts his big hands to my waist. "Sit on my face and let me eat you"

"Stop it." I gently smack at his hands. And because tears *are not* stinging my eyes for him, I open my mouth over his, kissing him, swallowing the last of that sentence.

I understand if you don't want to chance being with me raw. I get it. And shit, I wouldn't advise it.

He basically called himself dirty. And not the good kind. I kiss him deeper, relaying what I don't have the words, or the courage, to say aloud.

Sex, I remind myself. This is about sex. And pleasure. And forgetfulness. Don't let this turn into something else.

"I'm on the Pill," I murmur against his lips. "Are you okay with going inside me with no condom?"

He stares up at me, blinks, then slicks his tongue over his sensual bottom lip.

"Yeah, baby. I'm good with that," he rasps.

I press my forehead to his as I hitch my hips high, reaching between us to wrap my fingers around his fully hard and hot cock.

"Listen to me, okay?" I whisper, notching the head at the mouth of my sex. "I'm going to use you until my body hurts and the ache stops." I press down. Hard. And the tip slowly penetrates me, spreading me. I sink my teeth into my own bottom lip, gasping softly. Panting, I breathe one last warning. "Only this time, it'll be me who walks away."

His blue eyes glint, but I close mine and focus on taking him inside my body.

"*Fuck, fuck, fuck.*" He'd been big in my hands and my mouth, but stretching my pussy? He feels ten times larger, thicker and longer. He's a goddamn monster. "I can't..."

"Shh. You can take it," King murmurs. "You're going to take it."

I want to rebel against that thin vein of steel running through that command, but my sex must be a submissive or something because I swear, it quivers, relaxes, allowing him in another couple of inches.

"There you go. This pussy remembers me," he praises. Reaching down, he slides two fingers over my lewdly spread lips, rubbing them, spreading the glistening juice there down to my entrance and back up to my clit. "Mmm." He lifts those fingers to his mouth, and his tongue curls around the digits, licking them clean. "Just as fucking good as I remember."

Wetting his fingers again, he circles that engorged bundle of nerves at the top of my sex, and together we watch as it trembles for him, flinches from his touch. My body jerks with the jolt of pleasure that shocks me, electrical pulses rippling through me. And oooh, God, I sink farther down on his dick.

"King," I whine. Yes, honest-to-God whine. Because it's me begging now.

For more of his touch that edges pain and careens into pleasure. I'm at the point where pain doesn't deter me. I welcome it. I only need to be filled with him. Branded by him. Fucking split in two by him.

Palming his shoulders, I slide a couple of inches

off his cock and thrust down, pinning myself on his flesh like a butterfly on a corkboard.

"*Goddamn*," he grunts, his back arching tight off the ground. "Shit. Goddamn."

I'd curse, too, if I could speak. If I could draw air into my lungs. But my body is on fire, and I can't move. I blink against the pain that has pushed back most of the pleasure.

Breathe. In and out. In and out.

Yeah, not working.

"Dammit, Len." King mutters.

Then cool air brushes over my chest, followed by heat and a hard, wet suction to my nipple that zings pleasure so acute to my clit and pussy that it rips a cry from me.

Oh God. I clasp my arms around King's head, cradling him to me so he doesn't stop the wonderful, magical thing he's doing to me. He tugs down the bra cup on my other breast and his clever, musician fingers toy with the beaded tip, tweaking, pinching even as his tongue and teeth suck and graze its twin. It's almost too much, his lips, tongue and fingers. The pleasure swells, rushing in, and I'm swamped by it.

I'm mewling like that kitten he called me earlier, rocking against him, offering myself up to him. Not caring that the user has become the used.

"All right, baby." He pops my nipple free, giving it one last lick, then lying back on the ground, his hands cradling my hips. "Ride me. Fuck me."

I do. I do all of that. And more.

There's no more pain. Only the ravenous need that drives me to glide up his length and drop back down. To repeat the motion over and over. To dance on his cock. To pursue the ecstasy that glimmers right on the edge, just out of my reach.

Maybe I don't ride hard or fast enough after it. Maybe I don't want this moment in these woods where only lust and the two of us reside to end.

And maybe it's that last thought that scares the hell out of me and has me skimming a hand down my own body to rub fingers over my clit. With one tight, firm circle and his eyes on me...another caress...and another, I'm flying.

No, no. That's too pretty. I'm cracking down the middle, splintering, spilling. It's ugly, it's messy, it's real. And as King swells thick inside me, hammering away and spurting his cum deep, I can acknowledge this was a mistake. A selfish mistake that will cost me.

Right now, though, with his orgasm triggering a smaller, tighter one inside me, I can't bring myself to care.

Later.

Later, I'll care.

But not right now.

6

Lennon

"**Y**ou fucked him, didn't you?"

I cough, choking on a cherry tomato. Picking up my sweet tea, I down sips of it, glaring at Lena over the rim of the glass.

She didn't appear at all repentant as she bit into her bacon cheeseburger and arched an eyebrow. I scan Rise 'n Shine Diner, but no one else in the fifties style restaurant seems to be paying us any attention. Of course, that means nothing. They could possess amazing poker faces and really big ears.

"Could you say that just a little bit louder?" I hiss, leaning across the table. "Pastor Mays over at the church didn't quite hear you."

"Maybe you need to go on over to Paster Mays. I hear confession is good for the soul." Lena jabs a French fry at me, then dips it in ketchup. "Because you're certainly not confiding in me."

"I really don't want to have this discussion here," I mutter, stabbing my fork at the Romaine lettuce on my plate.

"I respect that." A pause. "It was the day you bailed on me and India, wasn't it?"

Groaning, I drop my fork to my plate and drop my forehead in my hands. "Lena."

"And that right there, ladies and gentlemen, is the classic posture of I Done Fucked Up." Lena leans forward and pokes at my forearm. When I glance up, she props her arms on the tabletop and narrows her gaze on me. "What happened to our pact? You were supposed to call me before you fell on the dick." When I groan and tip my head back, she pokes me again. "No, seriously, Lennon. That was our promise to each other. We look out for each other, remember? Well, while you've been indulging in the rock star peen, I haven't gone within a hundred feet of Ben."

I squint at her. "Why do you sound like the language in a restraining order?"

She waves a hand, brushing my observation aside.

"Totally coincidental. And stop trying to change the subject." She studies me, concern brightening her hazel eyes. "The last time we talked about King, you told me you were terrified of this right here happening. I'm worried, Len. Do you know what you're doing?"

Closing my eyes, I pinch the bridge of my nose.

"Here's where I wish I could tell you yes. But truth?" I look at my friend and slowly shake my head. "No. I thought I did. At the time, I convinced myself I did, but now?" I shrug a shoulder. "I just don't..."

"Can I ask you a question?" When I nod, she stretches my arm across the table, palm up. I curl my hand around hers. "What are you so afraid to admit to yourself?"

"I'm not"

But she squeezes my fingers, cutting me off. "Don't

be so quick to speak. Think on it. What are you so afraid to look at and admit to yourself?"

My lips part once more to deny being afraid of anything but then I close them. And think. Really... think. The answer isn't so difficult to come up with. It's voicing the answer that's a struggle. This is Lena, though. In spite of the teasing and shade we throw back and forth at each other, there's no judgment between us, only love and acceptance.

"I'm afraid to admit that I'm weak. Am I weak? Because my father treats me like I am. Did King see that in me all those years ago? Is that why he was with me in the first place and it was so easy to leave me? Is that what he sees in me now? Just an easy mark, a sure thing in the small town he's moved back to." I swallow hard. "So, I guess it's not really what I'm afraid to admit to myself. It's what am I afraid other people know about me. And whether or not it's true."

"I mean this with all the love of a friend who would not only keep your secret about where the bodies were buried, but would help you put them there." She gives my hand another squeeze. "If I hear some shit like that come out of your mouth ever again, I won't be responsible for my actions. And you're talking to a woman who allegedly set fire to a bag of dog poo on her ex's porch. *Allegedly*." She holds up a finger, and I snicker. "So you don't want to test me. Lennon, there's absolutely nothing weak about you. *Nothing*. You've survived loss, heartbreak, disappointment and you haven't become some hateful, bitter, angry person who allowed all of that to poison her. You're compassionate, sensitive, funny and so strong. There is nothing wrong with your backbone. It's not bent. And anyone who would try and convince you otherwise in an attempt to control you knows it.

They're scared you will one day fully recognize how much power you truly have."

She sighs, releases my hand and leans back against the booth. I briefly close my eyes, so desperately holding on to what she said, soaking it in. Wanting to believe it. *Needing* to believe it.

"I'm not here to make you feel bad about King. God knows I'm in no position to be judge and jury over anyone. You love who you love. But you also temper it with wisdom. Make your decision from a place of strength as the twenty-eight-year-old woman who has life experience, not the innocent eighteen-year-old. Innocent, Len. Not naïve. There's a difference."

I inhale a deep breath, hold it. Slowly release it.

She's right. It's been a week since the day King and I had sex. Since I dragged my clothes and boots back on then left without a word. Since I last saw him. I've been avoiding downtown or anywhere we could possibly bump into each other. The truth is, I'm doing just what Lena said—I'm not making a decision.

All my life, things have happened to me. Discovering and being devastated by Dad's affair. Mom dying. King's betrayal and abandonment. Even falling into a relationship with Justin because it was convenient. Though I chose to stay there for so long.

But now, I need to stop allowing my life to happen around me or carry me along. I have to plant my feet and decide which way those waters are going to flow. Being a spectator is no longer an option.

"Thank you," I murmur. "Thank you for loving me enough to tell me the truth. And for being my safe space. I love you, woman."

Her face scrunched up. "Now you just made it awkward."

I laugh, and maybe a weight hasn't completely lifted from my chest, but it's definitely lighter. Picking up my fork, I point it at her.

"Y'know, we really need to talk about this predilection for crime you've developed recently."

She rolls her eyes and heaves a sigh large enough to part my hair.

"Spoil sport."

King

"Okay, so I'm going to say it since no one else will." Kade, sprawled in one of the studio's wide armchairs, eyes me as he flips his drumsticks between his fingers. "What the fuck really happened in those woods?"

Even Rule, our engineer who came up to help us lay down tracks for a couple of songs we've been working on, turns around and looks at me. Mac, sitting next to him in front of the sound board, arches an eyebrow. And Gideon, who just returned from the booth, drops into the other armchair and crosses his arms over his chest.

Shit. I stand up and set the guitar I'd been strumming on one of the stands. Returning to the couch, I sink down, picking up my room temperature bottle of water. Unable to help myself, I glance at the state-of-the-art baby monitor that allows me to listen in on Gunner even out here in the studio. With a turn of a knob, I can even peek in on him up at the house. Not that I don't trust Matt—I wouldn't have him within a hundred feet of my son if I didn't. But, well... Yeah, I'm an overprotective father. Sue me.

"He's stalling," Gideon says.

"Definitely stalling," Mac adds.

"Which means something *definitely* happened in those woods." Kade hikes his leg over the arm of the chair, and swings his foot.

"I've only been here for a day and *I* know something happened in the woods," Rule drawls.

"You're all fucking hilarious," I growl. "And it's none of your business."

"Well, that's an admission if I've ever heard one." Mac shakes his head and props his elbows on his knees. "But what the hell. I go for a walk in this hamlet and"

Gideon snorts. "Hamlet?"

"It means village, small town. Read a book." Mac tosses a pick at him and Gideon deftly snatches it out of the air.

"I know what it means, asshole. I'm just wondering why you're using it like you've suddenly become a nineteenth century bard."

"You know, the sexual tension between you two is hot, but can we focus on King and who he got his *Hungry Like the Wolf* on with in the forest?" Kade interrupts.

Both Gideon and Mac flip him off but Mac shoves to his feet and strolls over to the built-in refrigerator.

"Oh please." He grabs a water and leans back against the wall, eyes narrowed on me. "We all know who he was with. The real question is how the hell he found her there and did all the dirt on his clothes mean what we think it means."

"That's two questions," I hedge.

Because I'm not saying shit about Lennon or the explosive sex that happened on that rise in the woods. Hell, it's been a week and I still wake up, sweating, dick in my hand, cum all over my stomach. I was fucking there and even I have a hard time believing it happened.

She's been smoke. Haven't heard from her. Haven't seen her. What had she said to me? She intended to use me and she'd walk away this time.

Well, she'd followed through on her promise. She'd walked away and hadn't looked back.

And the loss, after having been inside her after a decade, is like a limb amputated. She's not here, but dammit, I feel her, need her. But she's beyond my reach. And there's not a damn thing I can do about it. The height of selfishness would be me pursing her when I'm not just a bad bet, am not who or what she needs, but when I'm still choosing to lie to her. There would be a greater chance of all the planets converging than her father accepting me. And I can't put her in the position of having to choose between me and her only remaining parent. It would destroy her.

And so would discovering the truth about why I left.

For once, I refuse to be selfish.

"Do you think this is smart?" Gideon murmurs.

I glance at him, and he steadily meets my gaze. There's no judgment or censure in either his eyes or his tone. Just concern. And there's no way in hell I can be defensive about the question. He has a right to ask me that—they all do. They were in hell with me...because I dragged them there. And then they helped haul my ass out again.

"Do you need me to..." Rule jerks his head toward the studio door.

"No, you're good." I flick a hand toward his chair. "It's not like you weren't there and don't know what we're talking about." How many times did I show up at the studio high as fuck and unable to work? Rule has seen all of my shit, the good and the bad. Falling back against the couch, I look at each of my friends. "I don't know if this is smart. Getting involved with anyone this soon after rehab is a bad idea. But a woman I have a past with?" *The only woman I've ever loved.* "Probably not. I hurt Lennon. I hurt her and betrayed her. And I've never forgiven myself for that. I'd like to blame that guilt on my need to be near her, but I would be lying to myself and you. I want her. Whatever scraps of attention she'll give me, knowing I don't deserve them, I want her. And the other day," I scrub a hand over my head, dropping it, unable to meet their gazes as I confess, "those were scraps."

The silence crescendos, gaining speed and volume and finally, I lift my head. All of them study me with varying degrees of emotion. Curiosity, sympathy, even confusion. But no pity. And that allows me to keep looking into their eyes.

"What if one of those scraps is a trigger?" Kade asks, lowering his leg and twisting in the chair. Frowning, he runs a hand over his beard. "I get that there's unfinished business between you two, but there's more at stake here. And I'm not talking about us or the label or even your sobriety. Gunner."

"Yeah, and we both saw her reaction to him at the auto shop," Mac gently adds. "Not saying she'd mistreat him, but there's something...deeper there. You can't take that risk."

"She'd never hurt Gunner," I insist, probably harsher than I intended.

It's instinctive, my defense of her, and they don't know Lennon like I do. Yes, she's angry with me, but her heart is too pure to ever hurt a child. Every part of my soul can attest to that.

Mac holds up his palms. "I'm sorry. I didn't mean

any offense. Maybe that came out wrong. What I mean is, have you considered that being around him might hurt her? Her expression, man. Her eyes." He shakes his head. "That was pain."

I hate you because you gave another woman what you promised me. A family. Gunner could've been ours. Should've been ours. But you stole one more dream from me.

Fuck.

"She doesn't make me want to use," I say, answering Gideon's original question, because Mac's... I can't right now. It's just another reason why an "us" with Lennon seems impossible. "Being with her settles something inside of me. It's like finding the me I was meant to be before the drugs. The me I would've been had I never touched that shit. But..."

"But?" Gidon pushes when I fall silent.

I swallow hard, remembering my promise to be honest even when it costs me. Even when I'm afraid of it.

"Sometimes I wonder if I'm trading one addiction for another." And if Lennon would be more dangerous than any line of coke.

The phone next to the sound board buzzes, jarring in the tense quiet. Rule reaches over and answers it.

"Yeah?" Pause and a glance at me. "Yeah, hold on." Lowering the receiver from his ear, he jerks his chin up. "Matt said there's a woman up at the gate to see you. Her name's Lennon."

The tension in the studio ratchets higher, and Rule surveys all of us, eyebrows raised.

"*The* Lennon, I'm guessing."

"Let her in." I shoot to my feet from the couch.

While Rule replies to Matt and hangs up the phone, Kade, Mac and Gideon stand as well, studying me. I wait, bracing myself for whatever they have to say.

"I'll go show her how to get back here," Mac offers and exists the studio.

The converted carriage house sits back behind the house, which makes it a perfect studio. Easily accessible to the house if I need to get to Gunner but far enough away that we can have privacy to work.

"I need to finish getting my own house put together." Kade stretches and moving forward, slings an arm around Rule's shoulders. "C'mon. You can hang with me. Later, I can take you to this malt shop Mac keeps talking about."

"I think I'll head into town to see what your brother's working on," Gideon says. Then frowns. "We gonna have to fumigate this studio before we use it again?"

"Shut the fuck up and let's go." Kade barks out a sharp crack of laughter. "And they call *me* the asshole."

Shaking my head, I watch them go, and as soon as the door closes, I turn around, thrusting my fingers through my hair. What is Lennon doing here? My pulse beats in my temples, and I hear nothing over its incessant drumming. My heart keeps time with it like an ominous percussion line.

Shit.

Eagerness to see her mingles with dread about why she's shown up here. There can be nothing good about Lennon seeking me out. I don't try and fool myself into believing there is—the time for fairy tales in my life—and my belief in themdied with my mother.

Minutes later, the door opens and Lennon steps in.

A week.

That's all it's been.

But it might as well have been another decade. My

heart thrust against my rib cage as if recognizing its owner, and it's willing to throw down and battle to get to her. How did I endure a decade staying away from her? From rehab, I know there were several factors that went into my using. Loss, abandonment, low self-esteem, fear of failure. Numbing the pain had become a way of existing for me. And she was part of that pain. Pain I had caused and had inflicted on myself, too.

But now, after only weeks in her orbit again, I recognize something else I tried to bury with the drugs.

The loneliness.

The terrible, gnawing loneliness that has eased just being in the same town as her. Being with her, touching her, tasting her. It fills this hole that had been as dark, as bottomless as an abyss.

This is the fear that I confessed to Mac, Kade and Gideon. I can't make her my happiness, my crutch. That's exchanging one dependance for another.

And yet, as I stare at her, I wonder if I'm too late. Am I already addicted to seeing those chocolate brown eyes glaze with pleasure? Or to those lush lips parting on a scream or spread so prettily around my cock? Or watching her beautiful dark brown skin mist with sweat from the arousal I've stirred within her? Or seeing her come apart as her slick, tight as fuck pussy pulls and squeezes my dick?

Or feeling her heart beat against mine as passion cools and she curls around my body, holding onto me?

Yes. It's too late.

Which is why I should gently turn her around now. Tell her I might've been cruel ten years ago, but in the end, it was the best thing for us.

That's definitely what I should do

"I've missed you."

She hesitates on the threshold, blinks.

Well, fuck.

Mentally groaning, I step back, granting us both physical and emotional space. And time for me to get my shit together.

"Come in."

She enters, closing the door behind her as she appraises the studio. I'm quiet as she takes in the overstuffed furniture, the recording equipment, the booth and comforts to make this our home away from home. Crossing my arms, I watch her as she finishes her study of the area, fighting not to fidget like a fucking schoolboy.

And I loose the fight.

"As soon as I closed on the house, I had builders out here to immediately begin work on the renovations. Soundproofing." I wave a hand towards the walls. "We converted the living room and kitchen into a live room where we perform and record. That smaller booth in there," I point toward the studio where an enclosed cubicle stands, "is an isolation booth for Mac's drums and Gideon's amplifiers and speakers. It's also for those occasions when we include acoustic guitar on the record. And then this," I spread my arms wide, also indicating the sound boards, mixing consoles and computers, "is the control room. It's where the engineers record, mix, add vocals or effects."

I manage to stop myself from giving her a guided tour of the hall and the bathroom, bedroom and another bedroom we use for storage.

Because, shit, I'm babbling.

I'm really fucking babbling.

Lennon nods. "It's really nice."

"It's smaller than our place back in L.A. but it's state-of-the-art and suits our needs. I mean, sometimes we might need to travel back to record, but for now, it works." *Goddamn.* I pinch the bridge of my nose. "Lennon."

"Yes?"

"Can you tell me why you're here, because I'm sounding like a fucking idiot here."

She smiles, and yeah, she can't do that.

She can't do that and expect me to function like a normal human being.

"That's fair. I guess every time we've seen each other hasn't exactly been...amicable."

"I don't mind your claws, kitten."

The acoustics in here are amazing and I easily catch her soft gasp as well as the flare of heat in her eyes before she lowers her lashes and turns away from me.

"Can I take off my coat?" she asks.

"Whatever you want."

She unbuttons the dark red pea coat, then slides it off her shoulders. And I clench my jaw, trapping the demand to put the damn thing back on. But as she reveals her perfect body in a black sweater and high waist jeans that conform to her tits, hips and thick thighs like a paint-by-numbers drawing, my cock hardens and throbs behind my own jeans. It takes every bit of self-control I possess not to fist myself, bend her over that sound board, rip those jeans down her ass and pry into that three-sizes-too-small and utterly perfect pussy.

Spinning around, I retrieve my bottle of water off the floor near the couch. I don't turn around as I down ever last drop and order my cock to stand down, that it's not having her today. Yeah, he's not having it. And honestly, I'm having a damn difficult time accepting it, too.

"King?"

"Yeah." I toss the empty bottle in the trash can and, taking a deep breath, face her again. And pray she doesn't look down. "It's been a week, Lennon. And no offense, but you are the last person I expected to see at my house. I can't imagine this is a visit for shits 'n' giggles."

"No," she murmurs. "No...shits 'n' giggles." She pauses, her gaze seeming to search my face but for what, I don't know. "You have a gate out front. Did you have the access road secured, too?"

"I made the call as soon as we came down off the hill." Frustration churns inside me, and I rub a hand over the back of my neck. "Don't tell me that's what you came here to discuss—my security measures."

"I'm struggling, King. You'll have to give me a minute." She glances away from me. "The whole drive here I practiced what I'd say to you. I had it all planned out. But now, I'm drawing a blank. This isn't easy for me."

"Just say it."

My voice doesn't sound like everything in me ground to a halt. Or that unease has my chest in a merciless vise grip.

Wiping her palms on her thighs, she walks over to the armchair Gideon vacated and lowers herself into it. She rubs hands together and studies them. After several seconds, she tilts her head back and meets my gaze.

"When you first came back to town, I said I hated you. That's not true. I don't know if it's ever been true, because what I feel toward you isn't as simple as hate. Sometimes I wish it were. The way things ended with us, I never had closure. One day we were in love and the very next, you were gone. No reason and I had nothing but a letter that left me just as confused as your silence. I felt powerless because you took my choice, my voice. And I was so angry with you for that. Not just angry but deceived and betrayed. Because you, of all people, understood what it felt like to be abandoned by someone you loved and depended on. You knew how much it hurt and still did that to me."

"Len"

She holds up a hand, palm out, halting my apology. Because I'll give her as many "I'm sorry"s as she needs. *Whatever* she needs.

"No, I don't need you to tell me you're sorry. Sorry can't unbreak what you've broken and it falls a little empty when you're still lying to me. Because you are still lying, King. And again, you're doing it, knowing how I feel about it. Dad lied to Mom by cheating on her when she was dying from stage four breast cancer, and I had to be the keeper of that secret. And both of them kept the truth about how sick she actually was from me until she only had weeks left, stealing time I could've spent with her from me. It's the thing I can't abide, and you're hiding something from me. Even if we could get past the violation of trust, this..." she shakes her head, her eyes solemn, "this we can't."

She isn't saying anything that I haven't said to myself. Yet, hearing it from her? It hits different. Like a fucking sledgehammer.

There's shit I can say. I *am* lying. Knowingly. Deliberately. My reasons don't matter. Intentions paving the way to hell and all that. And that's where I am. Hell.

"So you're here to tell me that you don't hate me but you can't do this..." I wave a hand back and forth between us. "Whatever the hell we're doing."

Her mouth quirked at the corner. "It's nice to know I'm not the only one unsure about what's going on between us. But no, I can't do this either. We argue, I have an emotional break down, we fuck." She shrugs a shoulder. "I'd rather just take the arguing and emotional parts out of it."

"You're not—wait, what?" My whole body jolts as if an electrical current rippled through it. I blink. Stare. Blink again. Yeah, no. I still can't comprehend what I just heard. "Say that again."

She nods, her face the picture of calm and composure—except for the tell of her teeth sinking into her bottom lip. My cock jerks, as if those teeth are grazing it. I briefly close my eyes. *That* is not helping.

"I said maybe we should remove the arguing and emotion and just leave the sex." She stands, hands spread out. Her eyes are both sincere and hot on my face, and dammit, she can't look at me. She *can't*. But it's not going to be me who glances away. Looking at her is *life*. "I don't know if I could trust you with my heart again. Especially since I can't trust that you won't do the same thing to me since I don't know why you left in the first place." She inhales a breath, draws her shoulders back. Her gaze drops to my mouth and my lips are branded by that visual caress. "What I do know," she whispers, returning her regard to me, "is that when I'm with you, I'm awake. I *breathe*. I haven't felt this alive in ten long years. And I don't want to give it up yet."

I thrust my fingers through my hair, tugging on the strands. Lust sears me and, holy shit, it's a shock that I'm still standing and haven't crumpled to ash on the floor. Under that lust, though, skulks a voice that sneers, *That's all you're good for—a fuck.*

I hadn't been good enough to keep my father from drinking.

I hadn't been good enough for Lennon all those

years ago. Her father threatened me and my family just to keep me away from her so I wouldn't drag her down with me.

I hadn't been good enough for all the hangers-on who only wanted to be around me, use me, fuck me because of who I was, what I had and what I could do for them.

And now...

Still, knowing that's all Lennon wants from me...

"Scraps," I murmur.

"What?" she asks.

"Nothing." I shake my head. "When does this... arrangement start? Or end, for that matter? Or have you thought that far?"

"King." She takes a step toward me, but I reach behind me and grab a fistful of my hoodie and haul it over my head, dropping it to the floor. Her eyes widen, and satisfaction twists in my gut. While she stares her fill, I go around her to the studio door, locking it. "King," she whispers.

"Dates, Lennon," I remind her, tugging on my belt while toeing off one boot and then the other.

"I-I don't know. I guess when one or both of us wants to step away, it's over. No strings, no problems. And it starts...now?" My chest and hands hold all of her attention, and a fierce pleasure rolls through me. I have that, at least.

"Good." I stalk toward her, my belt falling to the floor next to my boots. "Because you're right about a couple of things. I'm not a good bet and I can't give you what you deserve. But I can make this pussy," I cup her over her jeans, and she cries out, her head tipping back on her shoulders, fingers flying to my shoulders and digging in, "weep for me. Might even make it sing, too." I lean forward, gripping the nape of her neck and holding her in place as I grind the heel of my palm against her clit. "When I put my hand down these dick tease pants, am I going to find you wet, baby? Are you going to soak my hand?"

She groans, vehemently nods.

"Thinking I should find out for myself," I growl.

Placing an open mouthed kiss along her jaw, I yank at the button on her jeans and the zipper. She turns her head toward me, lips parted, seeking a kiss, and I give it to her. Thrusting my tongue deep, I take what she freely offers me, sliding my hand from the back of her neck into her hair and tangling my fingers in the curls. Pulling her head back even farther so it rests on my shoulder, I fuck her mouth and without hesitation, dive my hand underneath her jeans and panties to do the same to her pussy.

I swallow her cry, disentangling my hand from her hair to yank her jeans farther down her hips, granting me more room to move. When she goes to spread her thighs, I nip her bottom lip and then her chin.

"No, baby. Keep still." My eyes damn near roll in the back of my head at the muscular suck of her dripping pussy on my fingers. "You're so tight I can almost believe I wasn't wedged in here a week ago," I mutter against her lips.

She whimpers, her nails biting my skin, hopefully leaving marks. Tomorrow I want to look at my shoulders and be reminded she was there. Same with her body. I thrust two fingers inside her. Pull free until only the tips tickle the entrance. Then plunge back in. Over and over, I pound my way in, corkscrewing my wrist until she's on the toes of her boots, trying to get away. Trying to get closer? The steady flow of grunts, pleas and sobs spilling from her abolishes the getting away theory.

She quivers around me, that telltale sign warning me she's about to blow. Not yet. I've been waiting ten years for *more*. And I'm not going another day without it.

I withdraw from her pussy, deliberately curling my fingertips and dragging them over her slick, silken flesh.

"King," she protests, lowering a hand to grab my wrist, to keep me where she wants me, but I gently shake her off. "Please."

"Stop it." I kiss her, licking into her mouth. "You don't ever have to beg me."

Kneeling, I remove her sexy-as-fuck knee-high boots and quickly strip her jeans and panties from her, too. Standing, I palm her hips and guide her backwards, maneuvering her until she's sitting on the back of the couch. Gideon's right. I'm going to need to get someone in here to clean after I'm through. But only because I don't want anyone else to touch or even catch the scent of her arousal. That's all mine.

Once more, I kneel on the floor and flatten my hands on the insides of her thighs, spreading her wide.

"Oh fuck, baby." I press my forehead to her leg, rolling it back and forth, pulling the violet and musk scent of her into my nose, my lungs. "I never forgot this. Never." I plant a kiss on one knee then the other, kneading her thighs. "But memory can't compare to this. How did I"

I choke off the rest of that thought because it won't do either one of us any good voicing it. Right here, her glistening, pretty, swollen pussy. These powerful, toned legs. The evidence of the passion we share. That's what we have. And it'd be greedy and unfair to even dream of more.

So, not only am I going to take what I can, I'm going to gorge on it.

On a groan, I dive into her.

Her taste explodes on my tongue, redefining my palate. I've dined in the finest restaurants, sipped the rarest wines, sampled the richest delicacies, and none of them compare to Lennon. Sweet, earthy with a tang that's pure desire, I can't get enough.

Flattening my tongue, I lick a path up her folds, lingering a minute to worship each one, draw them into my mouth, tease them. Every crease and inch of her receives my attention before I move to her clit. Pushing back the hood, I blow on it, savor the tiny quiver it gives, then circle it. Tenderly, at first. At first. Because there's nothing soft about the lust roaring inside me right now. Nothing gentle about the pounding of my cock that's demanding I put us all out of this torture. Fuck that. I want her crying, sobbing my name as she comes.

I want to break her pussy *and* her.

Shifting a hand lower, I thrust three fingers inside her, knowing she can take it.

"King," she breathes, one hand clutching my hair, holding me to her as her hips buck, riding my mouth and my hand, and the other pressed to the couch.

Her face twists into a mask of painful pleasure, and it's not enough. She has more to give me. I know this body. I've loved this body.

"You got more, baby. Give it to me," I push, shoving hard inside her, licking her clit until it flinches under my firm strokes. "Fuck me. Fuck my face and hand, Lennon. Don't hold back." I curl my fingertips against that smooth place high in her pussy, rubbing, rubbing...

A sob rips from her, and God, that had to hurt her

throat. But she throws her head back, her hips bearing down on me with short, rough jerks.

"That's it, sweetheart. That's it," I praise.

Her pussy clamps down on my fingers in a bruising grip, and I have to fight my way to ride her through the orgasm. Keeping a steady suck on her clit, I give her every bit of this release, still pushing, still demanding she gives me everything. Gifts herself with the same.

"Oh God, enough, please." She whimpers, shoving at my head and trying to close her thighs.

But hell no, I'm not having none of that.

"I've made a mess of you," I murmur, pressing a lingering kiss to her swollen flesh. "It's my job to clean you up."

And I take my time doing it, licking all the wet off her inner thighs, her folds, her mound. When I finish, I sit back with a hum, pleasure a buzz just under my skin, in my blood.

"Now you're the mess." She swipes a finger over my beard and holds it up, the tip gleaming.

"Mine." I grasp her wrist and bring her finger to my mouth, curl my tongue around it and suck it clean. "C'mon."

Tugging her from the couch, I head for the hallway, only pausing to grab my hoodie and wipe my mouth and beard. I lead her to the bedroom and we barely clear the door before I turn and remove her sweater and bra, leaving her completely naked.

"My turn." She swats my hands away from my jeans and undoes the button and lowers the zipper. Scrunching her nose, she tilts her head. "Do you ever wear underwear?"

I arch an eyebrow. "Are you complaining?"

"For the sake of expediency, no. It's very rock 'n'

roll of you. But later we're going to talk about this."
She chuckles, and my chest tightens to hear the
breathless quality to it. Tugging down my jeans to the
middle of my thighs, she sinks her teeth into her
bottom lip as my cock springs free. "Later."

Cradling the back of her neck, I draw her closer as
I kick free of the denim and close my mouth over hers.
Without breaking our kiss, I hike her onto the bed and
crawl on top of her, slowly lowering my weight. I can't
contain my sigh. Back on the hill, had been explosive.

This...

This is no less explosive, but it's so much more. It's
a homecoming.

Because I haven't been completely naked with a
woman in nearly a decade. Shifted clothes, jerked
down pants—enough to get in and get off. The one
time I did, about a year after I arrived in L.A., I fucking
cried like a baby. This intimacy belongs only to
Lennon. And as we lie here, skin to skin, flesh to flesh,
it's like entering a house of worship after a long hiatus.
Reverence. Acceptance.

Relief.

"Let me in, Lennon," I rasp against her lips. It's not
a demand; it's a plea. And from the softening of her
beautiful brown eyes, we both know it.

She tunnels her fingers through my hair, pushing
the strands out of my face, and studies me. I fight the
urge to duck my head, hide. But here is the one place
we don't have to keep secrets from each other.

"Come inside me, King." She brushes her lips over
mine. "Please."

I don't hesitate.

I bury myself in her. Just like last week, it still requires some work, some time, but not as much. And in
moments, I'm fully seated inside her snug, hot pussy.

Pleasure so intense, so decadent, races up and down my spine, sizzling in my brain before sending the signal to my entire body that it's in pure heaven. She's slick, dripping wet and her previous orgasm has only made her tighter around my cock. Tomorrow, my dick should be black and blue from her grip, and I'd tattoo every fucking bruise to keep a reminder of this on me.

"Let me know when, baby." I rake my teeth down the column of her throat, nip her collar bone. "It's all you."

"Move." She twists underneath me, rolling her hips and sending bolts of lust through me. I grind against her as if I can drive more of my cock into her sex. "Oh God, King."

Levering off her, I hook an arm beneath her knee and bend it back toward her chest, opening her pussy up for me. Tilting her hips up, I pull free of the clasp of her body, enthralled by the sight of my dick, wet with her.

"Look at us. Look at me fuck you." I glance up, making sure she's staring down at us joined.

And her expression... Damn. I almost come from that alone. There's awe, greed and lust suffusing her features. Those brown eyes gleam, and her lips, swollen from my hungry kisses, part on fast pants. Leaning forward, I cup her nape, supporting her as I slide back inside her pussy. Together, we watch her part for me, suck me inside, take me.

It's beautiful.

It's hot as fuck.

"Again," she demands on a whisper.

I repeat it, pulling free, pistoning inside.

"Again."

Each slow drag of her pussy over my cock is exquisite torture, and it's not long before she's undulating and writhing, demanding more, and I break. Leaning into the back of her thigh, I plunge into her over and over, pounding us both toward that ledge, that abyss. Lowering her leg, I haul her up the bed and flatten my hands against the headboard, using it as leverage to fuck her hard and deep. She wraps her arms around me, nails digging into my back, her cries muffled against my chest. I feel the moment she comes. Her pussy seizes ahold of my cock, spasming and milking me.

"*Fuck*." I hammer into her pussy, chasing after her, and I don't have far to run.

In seconds, pleasure grips me, and I'm exploding, falling after her, Lennon's name a prayer on my lips.

On my soul.

7

Lennon

I close the door of my car and round the hood, gaze on my childhood home. Funny how one day it can feel like home and on the next, it's like a stranger. And I'm a visitor. Not by choice. As of two weeks ago, the day I declined Dad's lunch...well, it wasn't exactly an invitation. More of a command performance. Either way, I haven't been welcomed here. Not for lunch or Sunday dinner or a casual drop-in to see how he's doing.

Until today.

Unease curdles in my belly as I climb the front steps onto the porch. Grief steals in underneath that disquiet. I never thought there'd come a time when there would be this cold distance between me and Dad. Of course, we've had disagreements before, but he didn't cut me off for them. No, this is different. And now, after a two week silence, I've been summoned. And there's no other way to describe it. He actually had his assistant call and set up a time for me to come to the house.

Who said judges were above petty?

I lift my key to the lock but at the last second fist it and knock on the door. Moments later, Dad opens it.

"Lennon."

"Hi, Dad."

A beat of silence passes between us and I have the urge to hug him, kiss his cheek like normal. But his shuttered eyes and formal demeanor discourage it. He's *greeting* me, not *welcoming* me. I'm a guest here, and that unease and grief twists harder.

He steps back and waves me in.

"Come in. Let's go to the study." He doesn't wait for my acquiescence but turns and heads down the hall, leaving me to follow.

Closing the door behind me, I do. When I enter the study, better known as Dad's home office, he's walking to his desk and rounding it. There are a couple of armchairs flanking either side of the desk, and I sit on one.

Dad lowers himself into his big, leather office chair and leans back in it, scrutinizing me. It's a tactic I've witnessed him use often. Quiet and that steady stare. Unnerve the other person into talking first. It might've worked when I was a teen, but not now. Besides, he called me here. I have no idea what I'm supposed to start spilling about.

We continue our visual showdown for several moments, and then he slightly straightens in his chair and clasps his fingers over his stomach.

"I'll get right to the point, Lennon. There have been rumors going around town about you. And considering that little scene at Hunt Auto weeks ago, I have no reason to question them."

That unease gels into flat out dread and it sinks to the bottom of my stomach like a weighted anchor.

"I'm guessing these rumors have something to do

with me and King Sullivan," I say, injecting a calm into my voice that I'm far, far from feeling.

"You know it does." His volume doesn't raise but the sharpness of the words scrapes across my senses all the same. "You haven't been very discreet, although I'm sure you think you have been. People have seen you going back and forth to his home. Leaving there early in the morning or late at night. There's only one reason for a woman to be at the house of a man like that, and I believed your mother and I raised you better than that. Or at the very least to have more respect for yourself than to be some drug addict's plaything."

Oh God, that hurt.

Using her mother was a deliberate, well delivered slap, and he'd used it for maximum damage. I breathe through the pain and the shame that tries to sneak in, infiltrate my heart, my conscience.

Closing my eyes, I push the red, pulsing ache away and focus on what I know. And I know the woman who birthed me, who raised me until I was fourteen had been the most loving, compassionate, non-judgmental person on this earth. And if she was alive today, she would want a piece of King for hurting me all those years ago, but she would never, ever look at me with condemnation in her eyes. She might caution me to be careful, but she would support me.

She would love me unconditionally. No strings. Hannah Ward had never been disappointed in me. In some of my behavior, yes. But not me. Her acceptance had been complete and without question.

Unlike Dad.

How dare he weaponize her memory against me.

Especially when he didn't even honor their marriage vows before she left this earth.

"Dad," I say, my heart pounding so hard I can barely hear my voice. "I respect you, and I love you. I don't want to say anything that will damage our relationship, and I need you to give me the same courtesy. So leave Mom out of this."

His brows slam down in a frown and he leans forward. "Lennon, calm down and don't be ridiculous."

"This is me calm. I haven't raised my voice, and I resent you implying otherwise. Your problem with my behavior is just that *your problem*. It has nothing to do with Mom. And it's beneath you to use her name and memory to drag an emotional response out of me. The same emotional response you want to demean me for."

His chin snaps back toward his neck. "Excuse me?" He rolls his chair forward, flattening his palms on the desk. "I'm your father, and you *will* watch how you talk to me."

"Dad, like I said, I don't want to disrespect you. But you summoned me here. And in the time I've been here, you've called me a sneak, a disappointment and a drug addict's plaything. It seems a little unfair that I have to watch how I talk to you, but you don't have the same rule. I'm your daughter."

"You are disappointing me." It isn't a shout but it echoes in the room like one. It reverberates in my head like one. It punches me in the chest like a fist. Only by sheer will do I remain upright in the chair. I mean, I knew this. *Knew* it. But hearing him say it aloud. My chest feels like it's caving in. "This man is no good. He's never been anything but trouble. Trash one step away from a jail cell or exactly where he ended up. Overdosing on some dirty hotel floor surrounded by other drugged out criminals. This is who you're screwing around with? This is who you'd rather be with when you have a respectable, educated, successful man like Justin who's willing to be your husband and not just use you like a toy until he throws you aside for the next woman? Because he will, Lennon. That's what men like him do. You can't really think you're special to him. He might have bought a house here but he's not staying. What is there in Pike's End to entertain him? And when he leaves, where will you be? With the reputation as King Sullivan's whore."

"Are you finished?" I ask flatly.

He's poked and jabbed at every insecurity I possess regarding King. It's like he crawled inside my head and pried open the door to every concern hiding in the dark nooks. Am I exciting enough for a rock 'n' roll star who has been with actresses, models, other musicians, all gorgeous. And King talked about moving here to give his son a stable, safe home, but after living in California all these years, could he really settle down here in quiet, boring Pike's End? What would hold him here? Nothing did ten years ago.

Not me.

"No, I'm not finished. Have you even considered the damage this causes to me? To my reputation? And what about your job? Do you think the school board will stand for your behavior? There's a morality cause in your contract. And the parents in this town will have something to say about the teacher of their children sneaking out of a drug addict's house at four o'clock in the morning."

"He is not a drug addict. Was he one, yes? But he's not one now. He's been to rehab, he's sober. He attends NA and AA meetings here in town. We all have pasts, Dad. But what we've done in the past shouldn't define our present or future. For example, if someone cheated on his wife, that doesn't mean they would cheat on a future wife or be deceitful or devious in other areas of their lives, would it?"

His face is stone, and we enter into another staring contest. I've never confessed my knowledge about his affair while Mom was sick; I kept his secret because I would never hurt her. But now I can practically feel him trying to determine the meaning behind my statement.

"And no one at the school has said anything to me about my private life because it's none of their business what I do when I'm outside of that building if it's not affecting my effectiveness as a teacher. And the only way they could know what I do with my aforementioned private life is if they're having me followed." I cock my head. "How about that, Dad? Because four a.m. is pretty specific."

"I'm your father," he repeats. "You and your welfare are my business. And when you're putting both in harm's way, it's my responsibility to step in and steer you in the right direction. Whether you appreciate it or not."

"I'm not twelve," I grind out. "You can give me your opinion, yes. And I have the right to take that into account or not. But to impose your will or your view over mine? You're crossing the line." I sigh and hold up my hands. "I don't want to fight with you, Dad. But who I'm with does not concern you. And if you can't agree with my decisions, that's okay, I understand that. But you can support me. You can decide not to penalize me for not falling into line."

"If you expect me to stand by and watch you derail your life, you're sadly mistaken. Now you have a decision to make. End this disgraceful behavior and get your priorities straight or you will force my hand. What will it be?"

Anger washes through me, temporarily dousing the hurt and disillusionment. Thank God. Because the fury strengthens me, while the other two have me wanting to curl up in my dad's lap and be his little girl again. And we can't turn back the hands of time. It's just not possible.

"An ultimatum? Or is this more of a threat? Fall in line or face the consequences?" I push to my feet. "Dad, I'm not one of your employees or a defendant in your courtroom. I'm your daughter. Not someone to control but a person you're supposed to love. Unfortunately, it seems I'm the only one in this room who remembers that. Do what you have to do. I don't give in to threats. I learned that from the man who raised me."

Turning on my heel, I stalk to the door. But his voice draws me up short.

"Everything I've done has been to protect you, Lennon. Remember that."

I don't reply, and I don't look back. It's classic Terrance Ward that he needed to have the last word.

Right now, I don't care anymore. My main concern is escaping this house before I break down in tears. And my pride demands he won't have that from me.

PART OF ME ISN'T SURPRISED THAT I END UP AT KING'S house.

As much as I've fought it—acknowledging how foolish it is—he's become a haven for me. In the last two weeks, the hours I've spent with King have been the freest I've felt in years. With him, I can be just Lennon, not Lennon Ward, Judge Terrance Ward's daughter. I can be quiet. Or I can talk. I can laugh. Or I can brood.

I can just...be.

And he accepts it. Accepts me.

That, for a woman like me, is more precious than a home in a nice neighborhood and a 401k.

I pull up to the gate, punch in the code that King gave me after that first afternoon in the studio and drive through after it opens. Usually, I text King before I come over and he meets me in the driveway and will take me to the studio or around to the side entrance of the house. My choice, not his. My insistence on our "relationship" remaining private, secret, though I'm sure his bandmates all know.

But tonight, I haven't texted him. And after I pull my car to a stop in the driveway, I step out and climb up the front steps of the huge farmhouse to the front porch. I raise a fist but before I can knock, the front door opens and King stands in the entryway.

"Lennon." He frowns, moving forward and simultaneously reaching out for me. His hand cups the back of my neck, drawing me closer, into his body. "What's wrong?"

The marked difference between his welcome and the one I received from my father hits me like a sucker punch to the chest and the air expels from my lungs on a ragged sob that scrapes my throat.

"Oh baby." He pulls me fully into his arms, holding me against his body.

His hand rubs up and down my back, soothing me as he whispers in my ear. I don't understand most of what he says to me because I can't hear over the cries that rip from my heart. I'm so fucking *hurt*. All I hear is Dad telling me how I'm disappointing him and the insults and the threats. What did I do that made me so...insufficient? Why have I never been enough for him?

"You are more than enough, Lennon. You are just *more*," King whispers, and it occurs to me that I spoke all those thoughts—or rather cried all those thoughts —aloud. "Get that shit out of your head. Because that's what it is—shit. You're asking the wrong question. What is it about him? Why does he have to be so controlling? Make you feel inadequate so you feel like you need him? That is insecurity, Lennon, and fear. He's the one who secretly believes he's not enough. But he can't admit it."

King cups my face and tilts it back so he can look into my eyes. My breath catches at the sincerity and... No, I lower my lashes. That can't be what I glimpse in his gaze. But then I'd have to admit to what is in my own heart. What I'm too afraid to confess. What I'm too scared to confess.

"He's frightened of losing you, but he doesn't know how to show it. Baby, I'll be the first to say I'm not your father's biggest fan. He definitely won't get my vote in the next election." I chuckle. God, how is that possible given the tight band around my chest and my bruised heart. "The truth is your father needs you. Possibly more than you need him. But instead of just saying, *I love you and I'm worried about your choices*, he goes the 'Kneel before Zod' route and demands complete submission and compliance. You're not weak, baby. You're damn sure not insufficient. He's vulnerable and feels threatened, so he's lashing out. It's not right, and it doesn't give him a free pass. But also know who you are. Beautiful. Strong. A light. And pretty terrifying. In other words, fucking perfect."

"I'm not perfect," I whisper.

"To me you are," he says softly back.

The constricting band around my heart loosens a fraction and my head falls forward, settling against his chest. His fingers tunnel in my hair, but it isn't sexual. He massages my scalp, comforting me.

"Everybody good out here?"

I lift my head and turn around to see Kade in the doorway, holding Gunner. His gaze roams my face, and there's no way he can miss the evidence of my tears. I glimpse the sympathy flickering in his eyes.

"You good?" King's hand slides to the back of my neck again, squeezing.

Before I can answer, Gunner screams and holds out his arms, his chubby hands straightening and flexing in a "gimme" motion. At first, I assume he wants King, but when Kade steps onto the porch Gunner does another of those death-defying dives that he did in Hunt Auto toward me. And like before, I automatically catch him, my heart clamoring.

His solid weight hits me, my arms instinctively closing around him. His scent of soap, milk and something unique to babies envelopes me, and I close my eyes, nuzzling his thick curls. This is just my second time seeing and holding him; he's usually in bed when I come to the house. I wait for that sharp shaft of pain that assaulted me at that first meeting. Yes, there is a dull throb but it's nothing compared to the warm glow that fills me at his bright blue eyes, rosy, appley cheeks and wide, sweet smile with its two teeth. He's beautiful. Absolutely beautiful and innocent. And he's a part of King. Do I wish that other part could be me? God, yes. But how could I resent this precious little boy for that? I can't. I just can't.

"Hello to you, too, Gunner." I sweep a hand over his hair. He babbles a whole lot back at me, but I'm pretty certain there's a "hi" in there, and I grin. "I'm happy to see you again, too."

He grabs one of the big buttons on my coat and goes to town sucking on it.

I glance over my shoulder at King, smiling. "Teething?" But my smile slowly ebbs at his intense, bright stare. "What?" I whisper.

"Stay."

There's more there. I can hear it in the deep, slightly hoarse tone that carries the same intensity as his gaze. I'm not sure what I'm missing, but it echoes inside me, and I shiver.

"Okay."

8

King

"Seeing Gunner again didn't hurt you like it did before."

Lennon's hand pauses in the lazy circle she'd been drawing on my chest at my observation. Her body stills, and for a moment, I don't think she's going to respond, but then she sighs and sits up, tugging the blanket up to cover her breasts.

"I need to apologize for my reaction to him those weeks ago. I never have."

"No, you don't," I say, shifting until my back aligns with the headboard. "You don't ever have to apologize for expressing how you feel. Or even feeling that way."

"Yes, I do. It was selfish." She folds her arms around her stomach and rocks just a little. "I held that beautiful little boy and instead of seeing his precious, valuable life, all I saw was what I was missing. What I didn't have. And yes, that's selfish." She releases another sigh and nods. "But no, seeing him tonight, holding him, playing with him... It didn't hurt me. He's so sweet and happy. And that kind of happiness only comes from a little boy who knows he's loved and he's safe and secure. You're a great father, King."

I look away from her because she can't comprehend what that means to me. How I worry if I'm doing right by Gunner. How I wake up in the middle of the night sometimes afraid I'm going to screw him up because I only had a positive father figure for ten years. For her to tell me I'm a great father...

It means the world coming from her.

"Will you tell me about how you found out about him? Were you...together?"

She's wearing a carefully blank expression, and I don't know if my answer is going to make her feel better—or worse.

"No." I shake my head. "I get how this is going to make me look, but I don't remember being with her. Even when we were across from each other in my attorney's office for the first and final time when she signed over custody of Gunner to me, I still didn't recognize her. We must've had sex when I was high, drunk or both. I was no prize back then. But neither was she. And I'm not talking about because she fucked a man she didn't know. I mean because she found out who my agent was and dropped Gunner off in his car seat at his office."

Lennon's head jerked back. "You're lying."

"I wish I was. The only way we tracked her down was the CCTV camera outside my agent's office. It caught her tag number."

"That's fucked up," she snaps, fury lacing her voice.

"My manager and agent tried to convince me to turn him over to child protective service, but I took one look at him and knew the truth. I let them run a DNA test but I took him home with me that day. Just weeks out of rehab and I became a father. Of a six-month-old. But he gave me even more of a reason to keep clean. I didn't save him, it's the other way around."

She nods. A small frown creases her brow, and her eyes grow unfocused. But after a moment, it clears. And she glances at me.

"What happened there? What were you thinking just now?" I ask.

"I..." Her hand flutters as if she's attempting to conjure the words but failing.

"Just say it, Lennon," I gently push.

"Right." She drags in a breath then slowly releases it. "Back in the garage breakroom you said you had looked back and never stopped caring. Was that..." She pauses and her throat works. "Was that true?"

"Fuck yes," I breathe. She blinks at the fierceness in my voice but I can't hold back. I *won't* hold back. There are other secrets between us, but this won't be one of them. "Not one day in the past ten years has gone by when I haven't thought about you. Dreamt about you. Fucked my fist to you. Closed my eyes and fucked someone else wishing they were you." She closed her own eyes, but I surge forward, grabbing her chin. "Look at me, Lennon. My truth is ugly as fuck. I've never pretended otherwise. But that's what it is."

"I shouldn't have asked"

"Yes, you should've," I insist, giving her head a small shake. "Do you know how it's possible for me to write love songs? You. You're the reason. I've tasted love before, drowned in it. Even after I fucked it up, I still had the memory to survive off of. It was so good, so strong, I could write about what I'd known. Did I look back? Did I care? If I didn't, I don't know how I would've made it through the last ten years, baby."

She stares at me, so still. So damn still.

Then, in a burst of movement, she knocks my hand away and crawls on top of me. Her mouth crushes down on me. And like we're back in that small clearing in the woods, she explodes all over me in a flurry of desire. Mouth on mine, hands in my hair, pussy rubbing over my cock. Then sliding down my cock.

We both groan. Then curse.

Then we slide into oblivion. Into pleasure.

Into each other.

PIKE'S END AT FIVE O'CLOCK IN THE MORNING HAS A different feel to it. It's like the town sits on the cusp of a place in between sleep and wakefulness, fragility and solidity. It's quiet, almost solemn. And in all the years I've lived here, it's my first time experiencing it.

Seems appropriate I would after following Lennon home to make sure she arrived home safely. Not that Pike's End has a high crime rate—I think my father and brother racked up the highest numbers—but still, I'm not taking any chances. I always tail her after she leaves my house late.

Still, like this time of morning, it feels like we're on a cusp, too. Something shifted with us last night. With her showing up at the house, with Gunner and then our conversation and lovemaking. Yeah, lovemaking. The fucking has been phenomenal. But for the first time since we were eighteen and twenty, we made love and...

Shit, I'm afraid to even finish that thought in my head, much less vocalize it.

But that doesn't stop that damn flutter from taking

flight behind my ribs. Flutters. The fuck. That's who I am now.

I grin. And yeah, I realize I'm driving alone in my car grinning like an ass, but apparently that's also who I am now.

The flashing blue lights and pulse wail of a siren catch me by surprise, and it takes me a few seconds to realize that the police car behind me is signaling for me to pull over.

The hell?

I frown and glance down at the speedometer. The speed limit is twenty-five and I'm going thirty. So technically speeding but nothing dangerous or something to be ticketed for. Pulling over to the side of the street, I lower my window and shut off the car. The cold November wind blows in, but I barely feel it.

Something isn't right.

But this is Pike's End. What can happen here?

Two police officers exit their cruiser and approach my Range Rover, one older, about mid-fifties or so, and the other younger, maybe a few years younger than me. The older cop steps up to my window, while the other hangs back.

"Morning, officer," I greet, going for pleasant.

"You ran through a stop sign back there. License, registration, and proof of insurance, please."

Okay, so either he resented working the graveyard shift or he resented me. Maybe both. But one thing I know for sure. I didn't run a fucking stop sign because there wasn't one for me to run. Still if they have nothing better to do than harass a so-called newcomer in town, then to hell with it.

"Sure."

Grinding my teeth together, I pop open the glove compartment and reach for my registration and insurance. Then, grabbing my wallet out the console and removing my license, I hand all three over to the office. He accepts them without a word and returns to his car. The younger cop remains and throws a quick glance at his partner's receding back.

"Hi, Mr. Sullivan. These are pretty awkward circumstances but I'm a huge fan. I moved to Pike's End about five years ago. Couldn't believe when I heard you'd moved back here"

"Wilson!"

Wilson winced, and even in the shadows, I saw red stain his cheeks.

"Sorry." And then he hurried back to the cruiser.

Snickering, I grab my phone, pull up the email app and starting scrolling through. There's nothing there I really want to reply to, or anything my agent or manager can't address. Closing it out, I head over to Instagram

"Please exit the car, Mr. Sullivan."

I jerk my head up and meet the older officer's steady, hard stare.

"What?" I ask. What the hell is going on?

"I said, please step out of your vehicle, Mr. Sullivan."

"Why? What's going on?"

His hand goes to his gun, and my blood goes ice cold. Sweat breaks out over my palms and slicks down my spine. Fear is salty and dirty on my tongue.

"For the last time, exit your vehicle."

Numb, I unlock the car and push the door open. As soon as I step out, he pushes me so my chest slams against the rear door and in seconds, he's hauling my arms behind my back and snapping on cuffs.

"You're under arrest for an outstanding warrant. You have the right to remain silent. Anything you say can will be used against you in a court of law. You have the right..."

The rest of my Miranda rights fade into the dull roar inside my head as he marches me back to his cruiser.

I can't just jerk myself awake and this will be a bad dream.

No.

I'm going to jail.

9

King

I went to jail.

For parking tickets.

I went to jail for parking tickets from ten years ago.

Fuck Terrance Ward.

"King, now you just got out of jail. Don't do anything that will get you tossed back in," Darryl Walker, my attorney, warns. His lip curls up at the corner as he descends the front steps of the courthouse with me, Kade, Mac and Gideon. "Apparently, merely existing in this town will get you thrown in the slammer, so step lightly."

He flew in from L.A. after Mac called him Saturday and told him I'd been locked up. His first impression of Pike's End has not been positive.

"This has nothing to do with the town and everything to do with the judge," Gideon growls, his frown so fierce that a couple of women walking past do a double take. Nope. Correction, they were just getting their phones out and snapping pictures. "He's got a hard-on for our boy here because he's fucking his precious daughter."

"Damn, Gideon," Mac mutters, rubbing a hand over his head. "Say it a little louder. The old woman over there, trying hard not to look like she's listening, didn't catch the beginning of it."

Said "old woman" turned up her nose, sniffed but didn't walk away.

Goddamn. Small towns.

"Two days," I snarl. "Two days that fucker had me in jail on some parking tickets from a decade ago. And he had those cops lying in wait for me. Stop sign my ass. I didn't run shit. And he knew if they picked me up on a Saturday, I would have to sit in jail until Monday because no courts are open on the weekends. That's two days away from my son. But he didn't give a shit about that. This was all about sending a message to stay away from Lennon."

"No shit," Kade says, his face the hardest I've ever seen. "And what are you going to do? Are you going to leave Lennon alone?"

I smile and it must look as mean as I feel because Darryl rolls his eyes and heaves a sigh.

"What do you think?" I ask.

Kade grins and his is straight evil. "Good."

"Great," Darryl drawls. "I should probably get a room at that little bed and breakfast I saw on the way into town. I have a feeling I might be needed." Then he smiles, and damn if it isn't mean, too. "And I'm looking forward to it."

I WAIT UNTIL LATE THIS EVENING BEFORE I DRIVE OVER to Terrance Ward's house. Darryl's been hard at work since we left the courthouse this morning, and in my hand as I walk up his walk and front porch is a manilla folder in my hand. Gideon, Mac and Kade's gazes are like physical hands on my back, and I had to emotionally blackmail them with Gunner to stay in the car. They don't like the idea of me facing Terrance alone, but as I told them, this is between me and him. He started this ten years ago, and now I need to finish it.

Terrance made me run then. Today's when I stop.

I knock on the door, and after a couple of minutes, knock again. His sedan is in the driveway, so he's here. But arrogant ass that he is, I'm certain he's aware I'm here but is making me wait. Just as I raise my fist to rap again, the door opens.

"I'd like to say this is a surprise, but it's not. Because inappropriate is who you are, Mr. Sullivan. You have no business being at my house and I'll ask you to leave," Terrance says, his cold brown eyes so like Lennon's but so...not.

"I will," I agree, then hold up the envelope in my hand. "After I speak to you. And I assure you, you want to speak to me."

He glances at the manilla envelope. "Threatening a judge, Mr. Sullivan? I see you have no problem racking up crimes."

"Threats, Judge?" I arch an eyebrow. "Me and this" I wave the folder, "can walk away right now and you won't see us again. You'll hear from us, though. That I can promise you. But," I shrug, "sure. I can go."

He studies me, and there's a glint in his eyes. His lips flatten into a grim line. Finally, he snaps his chin down into an abrupt nod.

"Fine. You have ten minutes. You'd better make them count."

"I don't need but seven, Judge."

He turns and strides down the hall, and I step inside the house, closing the door behind me. We enter a study full of dark woods and leather upholstery. I spare the built-in bookshelves, huge fireplace and heavy furniture a quick look, then focus on Terrance. He assumes the power position in the room, standing behind his wide, ebony desk. I smirk. He did the same thing when I was a sullen but scared twenty-year-old desperate to keep his brother out of jail.

I'm not that kid anymore.

I've made some serious mistakes in the last decade, that's for damn sure, but I've learned many lessons and have come into my own. I'm not scared of him, and I have so much more to lose now that I'm ready to throw down and fight. And fight dirtier than Judge Terrance Ward could even imagine.

"Well? Get on with it." He waves a hand. "You're wasting your time."

"Too true, Judge." I move closer to his desk until I'm standing right in front of it and I stare him dead in the eye. "First, though. That stunt you pulled this weekend. Beneath you. I don't know why I'm surprised. It's not the first time you've used that robe you wear and bench you sit on to get what you want. Not that you give a damn."

"Is this where you expect an apology from me? Still blaming others for your actions, Mr. Sullivan. If not for your behavior, you would not have been arrested. It had nothing to do with me. I just upheld the law."

"Right. It just so happened that on the night you daughter refused to stop seeing me after you ordered her to, I was arrested in a traffic stop at five o'clock in the morning for running a non-existent stop sign. What a coincidence."

He shrugs. "Sounds like an issue with the officers, not me."

"You would throw them under the bus when they were just following your orders?" My lips curl at the corner in disgust. "I don't think it would take that much digging to see who instructed them to pick me up on a ten-year-old warrant for parking tickets. As a matter of fact, my lawyer is on it right now. He's paid a thousand dollars an hour to enjoy it."

Terrance crosses his arms and cocks his head.

"I'm waiting for you to get to the reason you're here."

"Oh I'm at that point now, Terrance," I say, narrowing my eyes on him, and because I'm watching him so closely I notice the anger flash in his gaze at the use of his first name. He needs to get used to it. I'll never call him judge again because he doesn't deserve the title. "It seems I'm not the only one offended by your actions. My attorney is as well. So incensed, he's spent all afternoon writing this." I toss the envelope on the desk. "A grievance ready to be filed regarding the judicial misconduct and unethical and unprofessional behavior of Judge Terrance Ward."

Shock registers on his face. He blinks several times, his lips dropping open. For a moment, his gaze falls away from mine, and he sways lightly, but in the next second, his wide, solid body stiffens, and his mouth firms again. His eyes return to mine and they're dark with rage, and his smooth, deep brown skin pulls taut over his blunt features.

He sneers, and he scans me from the top of my messy bun, down my leather jacket and hoodie to the jeans not hidden by his desk. "You think that scares me? Coming from *you*?" The *you* reeks, as if he's just smelled shit on the bottom of his shoe.

I smile.

"Yes," I softly say, palming the top of his desk and leaning forward. "Yes, I think that scares you. You, Judge Terrance Ward, without a blemish on your record. Mainly because no one would dare complain against such an institution in this county. But you fucked with the wrong man. I'm not the same man whose brother you jacked up so you could use him as leverage to run me out of town. You counted on still being able to manipulate me all these years later, but you tipped your hand. Terrance, I hate to break it to you, but you're a county judge. A big deal here in Pike's End. But I'm a famous national and international musician with so much money Midas touches me to get gold. I've played in the White House and ate caviar-topped hotdogs with senators after I performed private concerts at their daughters' birthday parties. Who do you think will have their ear? Who has the most power here? You or me?"

I jab the envelope and shove it closer to him.

"And once that's filed and it goes public, and I start talking about a small-town judge who thinks he's the second coming of Jesus in a robe, it's only a matter of time before other people you've wronged start coming out of the woodwork. They'll all have stories about how the high and mighty Terrance Ward abused his power and position. My brother is probably just one case. And I promise you, Terrance. My Instagram account is bigger than yours."

His gaze drops to the envelope and he's struggling not to show his fear. I really shouldn't be enjoying this moment, but this bastard stole everything from me. Because that's who Lennon was to me. Fucking *every-thing*. So maybe it makes me petty as hell, but yeah, I'm enjoying this.

"If you care about my daughter so much you wouldn't expose her to that kind of publicity or ridicule. Or," his sneer returns, and I have to give it to him—he doesn't give in easily, "was your act this whole time just to get more of what you had of her at eighteen?"

I laugh and it's rough, jagged and angry as fuck.

"Don't pretend to be so concerned about your daughter's feelings now. I loved Lennon ten years ago. And if you had bothered to actually *see* me instead of look down your nose at me, you might have noticed. If you cared for your daughter, you wouldn't have kept what you did to her a secret for a decade. You would've balled up and admitted to her that you were behind sending me out of town and why. But we both know your main concern wasn't about protecting her as much as protecting your reputation. So don't give me that"

"You knew?"

Terrance and I stare at each other, shocked into sudden silence. In the deafening quiet, Lennon's voice seems to echo over and over.

I turn, my stomach bottoming out at the sight of Lennon in the study doorway. Neither Terrance nor I had noticed her standing there; we'd been too engrossed in our own argument. And now the cost of our negligence, our anger is the devastation on her face.

"Answer me," she rasps, stepping farther into the room. "You knew?"

"Lennon, I," I murmur, moving toward her, but her gaze is fastened on her father.

"Dad," she whispers. "You knew about me and King all those years ago. And you never said anything?"

Kade, Mac and Gideon appear in the study entrance, worry etching their faces, but I spare them only a passing glance. All I can see is Lennon and the pain darkening her eyes, pulling her mouth tight...

"Baby." I cup her elbow but she violently shakes me off.

"No," she barks, shooting me a look that cuts me straight to the bone. To my soul. "Don't touch me." Switching her attention back to Terrance, she continues in that same fury-laced, trembling voice. "It was you. All these years, I've wondered why he abandoned me, thinking it was me, something I did—something I wasn't," Jesus, that hurt. "and it was you. And you saw me hurting, and you never said a word. You could've alleviated my pain, my confusion, my grief at any time and *you chose not to*. Instead, you stood back and watched. Who does that to their daughter?"

"I did what I needed to do to protect you," Terrance thunders his same tired line.

"No," she shouts back, slicing her hand through the air. "You don't get to claim that anymore. Protecting me would have been telling me the truth. Protecting me would've been stopping me from beating myself up and questioning my desirability, my worth. Protecting me would've been respecting me as my own person and allowing me to have a choice. But you stole all of that from me for your comfort your status, your control. None of that was about *me*. It was all about *you*."

"Lennon, you will not speak to me like that in my own house."

"You're right, Dad. Because after tonight, I don't know if we will speak again for a long while. You placed your needs and wants above me. Then made me feel like a failure for the perfect storm you set up. I don't know you anymore. And I don't know if I want to

have anything to do with the person you've become."
She turned to me. "And you. You lied to me."

"I had to make a choice, Lennon. It was a shitty
choice, yes. But it was either sacrifice my brother to an
adult prison system for ten years when he was just a
boy or leave you," I hurry to explain. And I'm hurry-
ing, my words damn near tripping over each other because I can see I'm losing her right before my eyes.
She's standing there, but she might as well be drawing
further and further away. "I didn't want to go, but I had
to and I couldn't contact you or Leif's parole would've
been revoked. I had to, baby."

"You think I don't understand that?" she demands.
"I wouldn't have expected you to throw Leif away for
me. But you also didn't trust me enough to tell me the
truth. Not then and not now. Do you think if you'd
trusted me back then, I would've ran to my father and
told him? I would've kept your secret, I would've *understood* and stood by you. Even from Pike's End. But
you didn't. You didn't trust me then and you didn't
when you returned here. And every day since you've
chosen to lie to me. If you'll lie to me about this, what
else will you keep from me? And you even use the
same excuse as Dad. To protect me. You said I'm not
weak. But your actions prove you see me otherwise."

She pushes her hands out, palms out as if warding
me off. A shiver runs through her body, and I step toward her but she shoves her hands out again, harder.

"I need people in my life who respect me. Who see
me as a woman who can stand next to them when the
times aren't only good but rough and know I won't
fold or bend. Because I am that woman. I won't be
controlled by lies, good intentions, sentiment or even
love. I've had enough of that. And I deserve more than
that. For far too long I've looked at other people," she

glances at her father before looking back at me, "to give me that respect. When I should've just looked in the mirror. I'm starting that today. Goodbye, King."

"Lennon."

But she doesn't answer me. She strides out of the study, past my bandmates and disappears.

Out of this house.

Out of my world.

Again.

And this time I don't have anyone to blame but myself.

10

From: King Sullivan <kingdontgaf@yahoo.com>
Sent: November 21, 2022 3:26 AM
To: Lennon Ward <lennonforever1@gmail.com>
Subject:

Lennon,

Well, I hope this email reaches you because it's been ten years since I've used it, and I have no idea if you still do. Remember you asked me if I told the truth about looking back and giving a fuck about us? I guess I should start this off with some honesty since the lack of it is what got my ass in trouble in the first place.

I read every one of the emails you sent me after I left town.

Every single one of them.

Even the one where you told me go to fuck myself in so many words. I believe it was, Fuck you right back, King Sullivan. Yeah, I've even read that one thousands of times. And I'm not exaggerating. They're all I had left of you. I never blocked this email address because I hoped that maybe you might send me another email telling me to fuck off. I was that desperate for anything from you. I still am. Maybe one day I can show you my drafts folder with all the emails I wrote and never sent out. There are hundreds. After a while I stopped because it became too painful. But yours? They have a special folder of their own so I could pull them out and read them over and over when I needed to feel close to you.

Fuck, I need to feel close to you now.

But instead of reading them, I'm going to write you back like I didn't back then. Like I should've back then.

You're right. What you said in your father's office hit me so hard that I can't shake it.

I didn't trust you enough to tell you the truth.

But after sitting here thinking about it for the last few days, I've come to several conclusions.

Me not trusting you didn't have anything to do with you and everything to do with me. Your father and I had that in common. And goddamn if that doesn't pain me to admit.

All that time I didn't think I was worthy of you. The months we were together, I couldn't get why you —so beautiful, so smart, so fucking kind—wanted me. And I was waiting for the other shoe to drop. And your father was the shoe. It was almost a...relief. Don't misunderstand me. It wasn't a relief to leave you. It was a relief to have the waiting over with, to have my fear validated. I didn't believe you'd leave everything to be with me, the son of the town drunk who didn't have two shits to his name. And with your father running me out of town, I didn't have to test it. I didn't have to face your rejection. I was a coward, and I used your father as a convenient excuse to be one.

Another conclusion I came to? This might be news to only you, but I love you. So fucking much it hurts to be separated from you. My realization, though, is I don't want to be without you. Not again. I want the dreams we talk about. A family. A house. Christmases and Thanksgiving together. Waking up to each other. I want you to be Gunner's mother.

These past years have been a roller coaster of successes, failures, amazing achievements, incredible highs and humiliating lows. But through it all, they've been lonely because I've been missing the most vital part of me. You, Lennon.

I'll fight for you, for us. But I also love you so much that if you want me to bow out, I'll do that, too. I heard you in your father's study. I won't be the one who tries to control you with emotional manipulation and love. My love is yours, it always will be. It just is. And it's yours to do what you want with.

Yours forever,

King

11

King

I climb the steps of the St. Luke's Catholic Church basement where the NA meeting just concluded. Sometimes it surprises me how much I enjoy the meetings. If someone had told me that even five months ago while I was still in rehab, I would've asked what drug they were on. But attending grants me a place to release and talk with people who have been exactly where I am. Kade, Mac, Gideon—I love them and they're extremely supportive. But they can't truly understand like those who attend the meetings. And it doesn't matter that I'm King Sullivan. There, I'm just an ex-addict, walking that road of recovery just like them. Between the NA and AA meetings several times a week, I'm staying on track and I'm proud of myself.

Damn, that feels good to say.

I've come a long, long way.

More than that, I'm alive.

Pushing the door open, I step out into the evening night air. Thanksgiving's later this week, and it'll be my first with Leif in years. My first with Gunner, period. I'll have my biological and found family with me, including the Hunts. I invited them to spend the holiday with us since Leif usually spends it with his employer. Satisfaction and joy hums inside me at the thought of a huge dinner. There's only one person who's missing and who would make the day perfect and complete.

Lennon.

She didn't reply to my email. And part of me didn't expect her to. It's too soon after she's discovered both me and her father lied to her for a decade. But the ball's in her court now. I meant it when I wrote that I would give her space or even walk away if that's what she wanted from me. I'll never steal her choice or voice again.

It still hurts like hell.

Sighing, I head toward my truck, and I don't really notice the figure leaning against the side of it until I'm a few feet away. Frowning, I'm about to call out when the person steps off the vehicle and the streetlamp falls on her face. *Her* face.

Because it's Lennon.

A joy so fierce rolls through me my knees almost buckle. It's hot, bright and almost alarming in its intensity. I jolt to a halt. I have to because I can't walk. Can't move. Hell, that all-encompassing joy at the very sight of her? It might have incinerated the air from my lungs.

"Hey," I rasp.

She doesn't say anything, just takes another step toward me, grips the lapels of her short, leather coat and yanks it open.

I stare at her, at first not comprehending what I'm seeing.

I blink. Blink again.

Then I laugh. And laugh some more.

Throw my head back and keep laughing.

And it feels so good that I don't care if people walking by or coming out of the church are gaping at us.

This woman. She loves me. She fucking loves me.

Wiping tears from my eyes, I straighten and look at Lennon.

Lennon in a Bloody Sunday concert tee.

Smiling, she holds out a black marker to me.

"King, would you autograph my T-shirt for me?"

Grinning, I cross the space separating us in a few strides. I accept the marker, uncap it and sign my name right across her breast. Her heart.

Tucking the marker in my back pocket, I place my hand directly over my signature.

"I don't ever want to make any assumptions about you again, Lennon. Tell me what this means. Please," I whisper. And yeah, I'm begging.

"It means I've come for the gift you said you have for me. I figured out what I want to do with it."

It takes me a second, and only a second, to figure out what she's referring to. Her heart thuds under my palm, and my heart echoes that beat perfectly.

"What, Lennon? What do you want to do with it?"

"Keep it. Protect it. Nurture it. Treasure it." She covers my hand with hers. "And give you a gift in return. What will you do with it, King?"

"Fight for it. Share it with my son. *Our* son. Keep it safe." I cup her cheek, sweeping my thumb over her bottom lip. "Never break or abandon it."

She fists my coat and tugs me closer, rising up on tip toe, and I lower my head to meet her halfway.

"Don't ever lie to me again. Ever."

I shake my head. "Not even about whether a pair of pants makes your hips look big."

The corner of her mouth quirks and then she grins.

"Okay, we can negotiate."

Laughing, I wrap her in my arms and she throws hers around my neck. I take her mouth in a kiss, and damn, I've missed this. Our tongues tangle, and I reacquaint myself with her taste, the feel of her even though it's only been days. That's much too long.

I want forever with this woman.

And now we have it.

After so long apart, it's ours.

ONE YEAR LATER

Lennon

"It smells amazing in here." Strong, tattooed arms wind around me as a wide, hard chest presses to my back. Soft yet firm lips brush my neck with just a hint of teeth. Desire coils within me, pulling taut and hard under my belly button before spreading through me in a delicious, thick wave of heat. "I'm almost willing to admit this spread is worth letting you out of the bed so early in the morning."

Snorting, I tilt my head back and grant King a healthy serving of side-eye.

"Please. You might've *let*," I lift my hands from the gravy I'm stirring on the stove and curl my fingers in air quotes, "me out of the bed but not without a couple of orgasms."

"You're complaining?" he scoffs, his teeth grazing the curve of my ear.

"Do I look like a fool?" A shudder trips down my spine, and I can't stop my hips grinding against him. What can I say? My ass has a mind of its own. "You hoped to wear me out so I wouldn't climb out of that bed. I'm on to your tricks."

"I happen to know you love my tricks. Without them, we wouldn't have lil' Prince here."

His hand slides over my baby bump, cradling it. Warmth, like liquid sunshine, pours streams through me, and I tilt my head back again, kissing the underside of his jaw, his chin.

I'm happy.

That warmth is happiness. Contentment. Peace. Love.

I've never been so loved in my life, and the evidence of it sleeps beneath his hand. A baby, a life created by our passion, our devotion, our commitment to one another. Sometimes, it doesn't seem...real that this is my life.

Over a year ago, I'd been lonely in a dead-end relationship, in an emotional tug-of-war with my father, seeking his approval. And there'd been this emptiness that had resided inside me for ten years.

Now, I'm married to the love of my life, a proud mom to a beautiful, brilliant son with another on the way. While my father and I remain estranged, I have a big family bound by love if not DNA. And I'm no longer empty; I'm so full there are days I wake up in the middle of the night and stroke my hands over the strong chest under my cheek just to make sure this isn't a dream.

"I already told you we're not naming our baby Prince." I turn back to the stove, pick up the spoon and return to stirring the thickening gravy. "That would be a really odd choice for her."

"How do you figure? Prince was the great—wait." His voice hitches, stumbling to a halt. He stiffens behind me. A moment later, he reaches around me, removing the spoon from my hand and twisting the knob to turn off the flames beneath the pan. He turns me around to face him, his hands cupping my face, tilting my head back. "Her?" he rasps. "Did you say 'her'?"

I nod, unable to contain my smile or my joy.

"I found out yesterday at my doctor's appointment." The only appointment he's missed. "I've been trying to find the right moment to tell you. But after you got in yesterday..." I poke him in the side. "That was your fault."

King had arrived home late last night from L.A. where he, Kade, Gideon and Mac had played at a benefit concert. He'd arranged for a private jet to bring them back home so he could wake up next to her on their first Thanksgiving as a married couple. Just as he'd promised.

That's one thing King has been proving to me over and over this past year. He's kept his promises. He's shown up. He's consistent. And even though this coming year will bring more out-of-town trips for concerts and promotional appearances for their new album, I have zero doubts he'll always return home to us.

I don't just love him. I trust him.

He huffs out a soft laugh. "And I'm not at all sorry." And since he woke me up to bury his face between my legs, I wasn't sorry either. He lowers his forehead to mine, our breaths mingling. "Baby, we're having a little girl?"

I cup one of his hands and lower it to my stomach. "I think princess would be a better name," I whisper.

His eyes close and he shakes his head, another one of those soft chuckles escaping him. This one is a bit more ragged, shaky.

"King?" I ask, stroking my thumb over his cheek. "You okay?"

Once again, he shakes his head. "Fuck," he breathes. "I could really use a drink right now."

Since I've been with him this past year and witnessed how much he values and protects his sobriety, I laugh because I know he's joking. Or not. I'm just certain he won't take that drink.

I grin. "Payback is going to be a bitch."

He groans and then his mouth is covering mine, his kiss a hot brand that resonates in my sex and my soul. He claims me all over again with his tongue, lips and whispered words of praise.

"I fucking love you, Lennon Sullivan." He buries his fingers in my hair, tipping my head back. His blue gaze burns into mine, stealing my breath. "For giving me a second chance I in no way deserve. For being a selfless, loving mother to my son. For giving me the opportunity to experience fatherhood from the beginning—to experience everything I missed with Gunner—with our daughter. I love you, Lennon, for you."

I rise on tip toe and press my mouth to his.

"I have a twenty-six pound turkey in the oven and twelve guests coming over for dinner in two hours. How many orgasms do you think you can give me in twenty minutes?" I murmur against his lips.

"I don't like to put limitations on myself." He bends, sweeping an arm under my thighs and the other around my back. In the next second, I'm cradled against his chest and he's striding out of the kitchen toward the stairs. "Only my best efforts for you."

I laugh. And moments later when he lays me down on our bed, covering me with his mouth and body, I'm still laughing. And he takes it.

Takes it and me.

Takes my everything.

ABOUT NAIMA SIMONE

USA Today Bestselling author Naima Simone's love of romance was first stirred by Johanna Lindsey, Sandra Brown and Nora Robert's many years ago. Well not that many. She is only eighteen...ish. Though her first attempt at a romance novel starring Ralph Tresvant from New Edition never saw the light of day, her love of romance, reading and writing has endured. Published since 2009, she spends her days—and nights—creating stories of unique men and women who experience the first bites of desire, the dizzying heights of passion, and the tender, healing heat of love.

She is wife to Superman, or his non-Kryptonian, less bullet proof equivalent, and mother to the most awesome kids ever. They all live in perfect, sometimes domestically-challenged bliss in the southern United States.

Visit Naima at www.naimasimone.com. Or connect with Naima through email (nsimonebooks@aol.com), through her website, through her newsletter or become a member of her fabulous Facebook Street Team.

ALSO BY NAIMA SIMONE

Secrets and Sins Series
Gabriel
Malachim
Raphael
Chayot

Guarding Her Body Series
Witness to Passion
Killer Curves

Bachelor Auction Series
Beauty and the Bachelor
The Millionaire Makeover
The Bachelor's Promise
A Millionaire at Midnight

Lick Series
Only for Your Touch
Only for You

Other Titles
Flirting with Sin